2025

A NOVEL

John Standridge

Dedicated to

Lynna Ruth Standridge

Preface

If you have not first read *The Last Best Resort*, I suggest that you do so before reading this sequel. The characters that were formed in that edition are for the most part found again here.

As I began the sequel to *The Last Best Resort*, on a spring-like June morning in 2014, the DOW stood at 16,960; the Nasdaq was at 4395, and the S&P 500 was at 1967. As I resumed my last rewrite in 2020, the Dow was at 27,8450 and the Nasdaq and S&P at 11,130 and 3,382, respectively. Crash-worthy, perhaps, but one cannot predict the future. Wealth inequality, a large part of the morality play in which you are engaged in these books, has obviously gotten even more severe. Just sayin'.

The following part of the Forward was written in 2014, to put it in context, but it rings just as true as I reread it in 2020.

Wars and conflicts in Eastern Europe, Sub-Sahara Africa, the Middle East and South Asia; epic droughts and floods, global climate change, habitat destruction and accelerating loss of species; coastal dead zones, bleached coral reef nurseries, massive oceanic gyres of plastic, acidification and pollution, overfishing and warming; potable water scarcity; uncontainable spreading of Ebola, SARS, or some other virus; and a polarized 'Confederacy of Dunces' providing leadership are the newsworthy daily headlines, but one cannot predict the future.

-- June, 2014

The Last Best Resort, written in 2010, seems almost tame, given today's real-world possibilities that include the mass extinction of species, including our own, but one cannot predict the future. Please read the prequel.

2025, the sequel to *The Last Best Resort*, offers the antidote: a world in which our carbon footprint has been laid low by economic collapse. A sustainable society is crafted on Sanibel Island as an intentional community with themes of self-reliance and self-sufficiency, and personal responsibility balanced with social responsibility. Follow the developing stories of love and of revenge as the hurricane season, serial murders, and the struggles to survive all interplay.

Visionary Fiction is the literary genre that illustrates and demonstrates the process of growth in human and societal consciousness. Visionary writing has the qualities of prophecy -- it can be apocalyptic in imagery, or it may be predictive in its insights, or it may contain a core of moral truth. *2025* contains all three features. It is a society's journey toward self-actualization.

If our killer-ape species is to survive the Anthropocene, we best ought to determine how to balance our population pressures and consumption patterns with the finite resources of the planet, because time is of the essence. We are all polar bears now.

If you *have* read **The Last Best Resort**, my advice would still be to go back and re-read it. As we approach the year 2023, it is remarkable that fiction written in 2010 would still seem at least plausible today.

-- July, 2020

Cast of Characters:

Jesse O'Connell – 3rd generation Sanibel native, calm and capable, self-reliant, and independent, sails daily, everybody's go-to guy, Ph.D. philosophy, taught at community college

Beverly McMahan – unlikely heroine, common sense, educated, unpretentious, skilled and willing to do a variety of occupations in the service industry

Doctor Michael Wilson – crusty but highly capable medical doctor, background a mystery

Marti Leinhart – level-headed beautician, friend of Beverly McMahan, beach comber

Jennifer Marin – beautiful and athletic tennis pro, brilliant chef

Alison Swanson – playwright and actress, organizes local productions and cocktail parties

Jeffrey Rogers – former NSA intelligence analyst, cynical

Liz Forbes, Sanibel Island native, friend of Lucy Cochran, the Sheriff's widow

Greg Johnston – thoughtful and kind-hearted, hard working

Fernando Lopez – affable handyman, jack-of-all-trades, and spiritual seeker

Book One

January 1, 2025

"Happy New Year!" exclaimed a chorus of voices at the stroke of midnight. Friends had gathered at Alison Swanson's beach house to celebrate. Alison had assisted her fiancé, Michael, the island's only physician, during the battle of Sanibel. Michael Wilson had attended to many wounded, triaged as they arrived, in those dark destructive days. It did not matter to Michael whether a person was a Sanibel resident, a mercenary with Island Security, or one of Major Kipling Alderman's soldiers in the Army of the Association.

It was commonly believed that Alison and Michael's unselfish aide to Alderman's troops made the difference between Sanibel being burned to the ground and the outcome of some structures and areas being spared. Alison's beach house was large, befitting her years as an actress plus her divorce settlement. Alderman spared it out of gratitude for her kindness.

The lawn party was settling into conversations.

"2024 was one year that I don't mind seeing in the rear-view."

3

"You got that right. And I thought 2020 was bad."

"Seems like most people have a roof somewhere. What do you think?"

"Seems like it. I know it took me five or six months to clean up debris around a house I picked out and get it in the dry. But it is coming along."

"Same here, found a sturdy place with minor damage from the shelling. I will be working on it for a while yet."

Michael walked down the steps from the house and joined the lawn party. Alison turned and moved in his direction as he moved through the gathering toward her. They met at a picked-over food table, one of many they had set out.

"Tough crowd," smiled Michael.

"They do appear to have brought an appetite," said Alison. "Do we have more?"

"Some, but if *you* want to eat, you better get a bite soon."

"I am doing fine. Let's bring out the last of the food trays."

As Michael and Alison passed through groups of friends co-mingling, they greeted new friends as well. They engaged in conversations along the way. As they approached the beach house, they saw Jesse and Beverly.

Jesse stopped Michael to catch him up on the repair and clean-up efforts. Alison stepped past them and stopped with Beverly. "Hey, You," she greeted. "What's up?"

"Well…" teased Beverly. "I'm late."

"No, I saw you earlier. You weren't late."

"*Alison*," Beverly smiled as she fixed her gaze on her friend. "*I'm Late!*"

"Oh!" Alison's eyes got wide then crinkled in a smile. They hugged. "Does Jesse know?"

"I was trying to wait to be sure. Plus, you know how this is a risky time."

"Well don't wait too long," Alison warned. "Jesse would want to know."

"I know. I know." Beverly was quiet until she wasn't. "I will."

"Jesse," said Michael. "I have seen a broad range of patients this year – broken bones to broken spirits."

"Broken people with broken dreams, devastation everywhere," agreed Jesse.

"One thing that I am hearing is story after story about how you came through for this one or that one – repairing roofs, doing plumbing, holding hands and listening."

"Yeah, I'm lucky that Beverly and I are in a position to help out, a lot like you and Alison. What we don't have is structure. We are not organized. We need vision."

"Well, I can tell you this. It is appreciated, what you have been doing for people," said Michael. "It's very much appreciated."

"Thanks."

"We need to get this crowd fed," Michael said to Alison who was still in animated discussion with Beverly.

As they left to get more food trays, Alison called back, "Don't wait too long."

Jesse asked Beverly what she meant by that, "Don't wait too long for what?"

"I will tell you when we get home."

"I'm ready to go," he suggested.

January 14, 2025

"You know? I've been thinking."

"Oh? What about?"

Neither was really awake, their voices were muffled by Morpheus, Hypnos, and pillows.

"I was thinking that if we are going to have children, then we ought to get married."

"Is that a marriage proposal?"

"It might be."

"OK then. I accept."

"OK then."

.   .   .   .   .

The next morning Jesse awakened gradually, in and out of dream states. Beverly was nowhere to be seen; *probably in the gardens*, he thought.

When Jesse did get up, he planted his bare feet on the cool Italian porcelain tile and reflected on Brady Chapman. Jesse rarely gave thought to the assassin who previously built and owned the house that he and Beverly now occupied, except to appreciate his choices of fine building materials. Jesse found his Carhartt shorts and pulled them on while he looked about for a clean shirt.

Jesse slid open the large glass door and was greeted by a warm breeze. He pushed into the light headwind, rounded the corner and found Beverly on the patio. She had a small fruit bowl of apples and cantaloupes and smiled up at him as if she were willing to share her breakfast. He sat across from her as she poured him a fresh cup of coffee.

"Good morning young lady," said Jesse cheerily.

"Good morning, fine sir," replied Beverly. "Did I just dream it or did we get married last night?"

"I'm not sure myself," said Jesse with a grin. "But I do believe that you agreed to something of that nature. Maybe we should look around for some kind of document."

"I already did," she lied.

They sipped their coffee and ate bites of fruit in their common warm comfortable silence. When Jesse did speak he startled every rose petal out of her matrimonial reverie. "I gave a thought to Brady this morning."

"Our benefactor."

"Our benefactor," agreed Jesse.

"I liked Brady," mused Beverly.

"I know. I did as well," agreed Jesse. "But he sure thought highly of you as well. That is clear enough."

"Yes, I suppose so. We had some good conversations. There was a kindness between us, and I think there was a mutual intellectual appreciation as well. It's sad that he didn't come back. He had hinted that it was his last mission," said Beverly wistfully.

"He was enough of a warrior," reflected Jesse, "that I doubt he would have survived the invasion of Sanibel. But I agree it's sad that he is no longer with us."

More silent reflection ensued. This time it was Beverly's turn to break it. "What time do we need to be at the town hall meeting?"

"One o'clock, maybe 1:30. The meeting starts at two but we should get there early in order to gauge the mood. I want to get a sense of how everyone is doing and how they are feeling about everything." Jesse paused as if reflecting on the significance of the meeting, the first large gathering to occur since Sanibel was invaded and plundered by Alderman's troops over a year ago. "Do you think they will need me?"

"The people of Sanibel?" Beverly asked rhetorically. "Yes. Yes, I do."

.　　　.　　　.　　　.　　　.

Even before they arrived at the town hall, Jesse and Beverly encountered a dozen or more friends and neighbors who were also migrating toward the meeting place. These survivors were traveling faster or slower depending on their age or condition. A few were wounded and healing slowly over the year since the battles. Some were resolute: some were despondent. Most were traumatized to some degree or another and many appeared confused or dazed. One thing they all had in common – they were all survivors

Beverly gave Jesse's hand a quick squeeze when they saw Alison coming down a side street toward them. She smiled and they slowed to wait for her to join them. "They've all lost so much," said Alison as she approached them. Her face, ironically, showed both a sweet smile and a pained and furrowed brow which said, "poor dears".

"Everything!" agreed Beverly.

"Hello, Alison," said Jesse. "How are *you* doing?"

"I'm doing okay, Jesse. How about the two of you?"

"We're actually doing better than okay, Alison," said Beverly cheerfully. She stretched her left hand towards Alison as if to show off her imaginary ring.

"Jesse proposed?" asked Alison brightly.

"He did," Beverly added brightly. "He may have been talking in his sleep, but I heard it loud and clear."

"Oh, honey, congratulations. How brave of you – both of you," reflected Alison. "No, not brave,

11

just *right*. This is really the right thing to do. Good job, you two. This is really good news."

"Thanks. We think so too, but maybe not for the same reasons as you."

Jesse piped in supportively. "We're in love."

"Of course you are," smiled Alison who appreciated the fact that Jesse could boil the news down to its essence – the only reason that mattered to him and Beverly. Alison felt a little chagrined that she had thought more about what the life-affirming news of the marriage would mean to the crippled Sanibel community, and less about what it meant to Jesse and Beverly. She smiled and hugged them both. It was time to walk on.

．　　．　　．　　．　　．

The town square, the real estate in front of the bombed-out town hall, was alive with activity. It reflected the hunger of the citizenry for social intercourse, for human contact and for a chance to start over. Jesse scanned the crowds. He examined their faces and felt their anxiety. The people were insecure and uncertain. He listened to their conversations taking place in groups of three or twelve. The stunned citizens of Sanibel were gathering in small groups to take stock of how everyone was doing. Some were more traumatized than others; and with some, the damage seemed irrevocable. The more functional ones were taking stock of island resources, trying to determine if they had the means to sustain the community. Nowhere did Jesse hear a coherent plan, a vision for the future, a long-range strategy or even a short-term plan. No leaders were coming forth.

Jesse spotted Dr. Wilson and made his way toward him. Michael Wilson was standing among a small crowd by the *Keystone*, the slender chrome statue that had stood for decades outside the library entrance. How Alderman's missiles had leveled the town hall and totally spared the library was a testament to satellite-based guidance systems.

"How are you doing, Michael?" Jesse was concerned for the welfare of his friends as much or more than he was for everybody else on the island.

"Not too bad myself, Jesse, but it's really rough out there. At first it was just the wound care – burns, abrasions, and a few fractures. Then there were the withdrawal syndromes – opiates mainly. A lot of people were feeling the pain. Now it seems like everyone has PTSD – posttraumatic stress. This has become one stressed-out community. Even the childbirth can't seem to come out right. I had a woman last Tuesday with shoulder dystocia. I had to corkscrew the baby out – rough night."

"Well don't lose that skill, although I hope you won't need it for any complications. Beverly and I have this Planned Parenthood thing happening."

"I had just heard. Alison told me."

"News really does travel fast. Beverly and I just told her about our wedding plans 30 minutes ago."

"What are we going to do with this crowd?" asked Wilson. "Somebody must've called this meeting. It looks like half the island is going to show up."

"I don't know, Michael. I heard about it the same as you. I may have mentioned the idea to someone, but I'm not the organizer. Do you have any ideas where we go from here?" asked Jesse.

"Maybe a few," replied Wilson. "For one thing we know that Sanibel is fertile cropland. Before there ever was a causeway, this island was tomato farms. This soil will grow all the fruits and vegetables that we need to survive. It might take some motivation to get people to pull together, but I know these people and they are good folk. I believe we can get it done."

"I do too, Michael," Jesse assured him. "I do too. It is going to take some organization. But I believe that we can all pull together for the common good. I have been thinking about it. Remember when Fernando and Greg left Sanibel to go to The Farm in Tennessee? That place is what they call an intentional community. That is not a bad idea for this day and time. Maybe we should consider making Sanibel a co-op along those lines."

"That's not a bad idea," Wilson agreed. "It is actually something that we could get started on right away and continually fine tune and improve the process."

Dozens of people had migrated toward Michael and Jesse as they held their discussion at the *Keystone* statue in front of the library. There were murmurs of agreement with every sentence uttered. Dr. Wilson was too valuable as the island's only physician to be enlisted as their leader. Jesse, on the other hand, was not only widely respected and liked, but he had time and resources. Leadership was never something that Jesse sought. He did, however, recognize the need, and as the crowd grew and focused their attention toward him and the good doctor, he reluctantly rose to the challenge.

One of the striking features of leadership is how often the people who become leaders don't wish to be. When God first comes to Moses at the burning bush, Moses contrives a series of excuses and asks God to simply choose someone else. The story of Jonah tells of a prophet who literally tries to flee from God only to be swallowed by a large fish that spits Jonah out on to dry land to prophesy and save the city of Nineveh. They and many others who are hesitant to become leaders, once in the position of leadership, serve effectively and often with astonishing devotion. The irony is that reluctance in the face of a great task is the natural reaction of a healthy spirit, and that pursuing leadership is often a perversion of ego.

"Speak louder," someone in the back yelled out.

"Can you hear me now?" Jesse yelled back.

"Yes, but can you fill us in?" came back the response.

"Give me a little space and I'll see what I can come up with," agreed Jesse.

By now Beverly had joined them and the three of them perched on some nearby rubble. The crowd fanned out and focused their attention on Jesse. As the murmuring got quiet, Jesse addressed the crowd.

"Friends," Jesse began. "It has been hard on us. Many of us have lost our homes. Some of us have found new places to stay. Most of us have lost more than our valuables. We have lost good friends, loved ones and family. We have lost a way of life."

"Now the new time is upon us. Now we must survive or die. We must take care of ourselves and of each other. Now we must refashion and reshape our Sanibel community. It is totally up to us. No one is going to do this for us."

"As a child I was told that the Chinese symbol for crisis is the same symbol as the one for opportunity. We definitely have a crisis. It is up to us to turn it into an opportunity. We can do this – together."

"When an opportunity is available to all, it is then that creativity is most apt to flourish, since everyone can respond to it in their own time and in their own way. We have resources. We have a sea that still has fish. We have soil that is fertile. We have golf courses that are no longer needed for games but *are* needed for crops. We have a community of warm and kind spirits, of able bodies and eager intentions, and we have purpose."

"Our desalinization plant with its reverse osmosis technology gives us good water. We still get our electricity from the mainland, and if we lose that we can find ways to make our own. We should begin now to harvest the wind, the tides, and the sun toward that end."

"There are a lot of people here today. That tells me that the people of this island are ready, willing and able to get back on their feet and make a new life in this place. Am I right? Are you with me?"

The crowd burst into a roar of "yes", prolonged and deafening, and born of the pent-up needs, fears and anguish. The roar continued until a small group began and the whole crowd took up a chant of "Jesse... Jesse... Jesse... Jesse."

Jesse was taken aback. If he was reluctant to serve in the past, he was fearful of this new adulation born of fear and desperation. All he wanted was a small happy family – Beverly and a child or two. Creating expectations during desperate times promoted the goal of a happy ending. The good people of Sanibel were still a product of a philosophy of American Exceptionalism. Their lives were okay when things went well, but there clearly was a horribly unfamiliar void now that things had gone badly. The pendulum could swing the other way quickly. The love and support for Jesse could become disappointment and retribution if things did not turn out the way one would hope for and expect. It would not be easy creating a new society that required the hard work and cooperation of all. Jesse was not sure that he was up to the task of bringing these people together, but he knew that he had to try.

"Work with me and we can do this," said Jesse in a firm voice that hid his uncertainty. "Stand with me and we will make Sanibel a community to be proud of. It may be that true courage is to see the world as it is and to love it still. Sustainable ways will mean recovering the best qualities of humankind – of cooperation rather than dominance, stability rather than growth, and concern for the well-being of all rather than some ill-conceived virtue of selfishness."

"Our circumstances on Sanibel are unique. So too must the task ahead of us be unique. We will relearn how to do things with our own hands. We have the time. We have the will. We have the means. We have abundant natural resources. We will pull our families and community together to raise happy and well-adjusted children. We will merge that good grain of human nature with the bounty of our island's good nature. Everywhere there will be the opportunity for healthy work that strengthens ties between us, one individual with another, and strengthens our bonds between us and nature. We will respect the land. We will respect the sea. And they in turn will nurture and nourish us. It is a new life before us. Do not be afraid. We will seize this opportunity and make the very best of it."

"Here is how we begin. This is a big crowd. I want you to divide left and right: make an aisle down the middle."

The crowd divides into two halves.

"Good," continued Jesse. "Now, each half divide into three groups – a back group, a middle group and a front group. Good. Now, each of you six groups, choose one person to represent you. This will be our new counsel. The new council will meet tomorrow morning at 10, in the meeting room just beyond the elevator. Everybody else can be looking for tools that are serviceable, bicycles that are not damaged, and other community property that can help us fish and grow crops, and more than survive – *thrive!*"

The crowd erupted with cheers, with newfound hope, and with determination. They did as instructed, eager for direction and purpose, and began the process of choosing a truly democratic leadership. One by one reluctant heroes emerged, listened to stories of hardship, and took the pulse of the people. One by one the chosen representatives worked their way to where Michael and Jesse were standing. They were listening to the concerns of one individual and then another. They were feeling the press of the crowd and the pressure of the moment. Only when all six representatives had been selected, and had identified or introduced themselves did

Michael, Jesse, Alison and Beverly start working their way back home.

"How does it feel?" Beverly asked Jesse when they were alone.

"Heavy," he replied. "Burdensome. Scary. Nothing I would've wanted."

"Yeah," she agreed. "Nothing we needed, but something that had to be done. We will get through this together," Beverly added, "and Sanibel will be the better for it."

"Well that's heavy," said Jesse, but he was grinning as he pulled her toward him.

"We'll see who's heavy," she smiled back at him.

January 15, 2025

Beverly's dulcet voice sung Jesse awake. "Wake-up, Sleepyhead. You have a 10 o'clock meeting at the library this morning."

Jesse was not yet ready to get up. Their morning lovemaking had been energetic, and they had fallen back asleep in each other's arms. His dreams were elsewhere and his focus was certainly not on making Sanibel functional, safe and self-sustaining.

Jesse's comfort level and sense of satisfaction were both at a remarkably high point. He had lived alone on his sailing yacht, *Serenity*, for so many years that the luxury of living with the woman he loved and in a home that would exceed anyone's dreams was making him softly domesticated. Moreover, his personal and physical comforts were making him spiritually and morally uncomfortable. So many of his friends and neighbors were in dire straits, devastated by their losses, and were in such obvious emotional pain that he wondered how he could represent them honestly. And yet it was just such self-awareness that might allow him to rise to the occasion and make something valuable out of the recent tragedy.

Jesse showered quickly, found his Carhartt shorts, a shirt and some sandals, and lingered over the breakfast that Beverly had ready. The fresh fruit was tasty as always, but Jesse was aware of the absence of fresh baked bread. Supplies and availability of many items that they once took for granted was one of the first agenda items the Council would need to address this morning.

Jesse pedaled the Litespeed bicycle toward Periwinkle. He appreciated the Siena for its lightweight titanium frame and its high-end components. With apologies to the communal

24

sensibilities of the island, he had appropriated it to his own needs. It was his favorite bike.

Jesse turned left onto Periwinkle and picked up speed as he shifted the Shimano Ultegra gears. He felt as if he were flying as he maneuvered between the cratered reminders of the artillery shelling. There was still plenty of smooth asphalt for bicycling, but it would take some serious roadwork before automobile traffic returned. Jesse was thinking that was not such a bad thing. Resources were too scarce to permit the return of a petrochemical culture. If road repairs came up as an agenda item at the council meeting, Jesse thought that he might just recommend converting the craters to planting areas. It would beautify the areas, create a useful activity for idle hands, and would help ensure that no one stepped into one of these holes and broke an ankle. But Jesse was having other thoughts as well. There were many matters of greater urgency that would be itemized higher on the agenda. He had met his Counsel team when they had introduced themselves after the selection process the day before. It was an interesting mix of people. The organization of the island toward a self-sustaining cooperative would be challenging.

It was a short bike ride and Jesse arrived early at the library. Michael Wilson was already there; so was Barefoot Chuck. Barefoot Chuck was an interesting choice for a representative. He looked older than he was due to a lifetime of exposure to the sun, mostly on a fishing boat. In truth he was probably no older than Dr. Wilson.

The others arrive singly or in pairs. Bert Krepazhski had peddled in from Captiva. Bert was a multitalented individual who was probably chosen because he was the plant manager at the Island Water Plant. He would also have useful ideas and insights for many of the maintenance challenges that lay ahead.

Jeffrey Rogers walked up to the growing group. Jesse glanced at him, caught his gaze momentarily then refocused on the others. Jesse no longer trusted or respected Jeffrey after that night when several bottles of wine had led him to reveal his MOAS – his Mother of All Secrets. Rogers had been an NSA intelligence agent. After he left the agency, he became rich arranging arms shipments that contributed to the genocide in Somalia and the chaos of post war Iraq. Still, Jesse was willing to give him the opportunity to redeem himself and serve the common good. He had major skills, experience and mainland contacts that could prove to be very useful. The more Jesse reconsidered the more he recognized that Jeffrey would be useful and even needed.

Liz Forbes and Mercedes Phillips arrived together. They were animated in their discussions of common friends and interests. Both were attractive women in their mid-40s. Both were artists.

Last to arrive was Lucy Cochran, the ex-sheriff's widow. John Cochran had been Jesse's closest friend for several years, his confidant and poker companion. Jesse left the others to walk towards Lucy as she approached. He had seen her briefly the day before, but they had not had a chance to talk since before the invasion.

"How are you holding up?" began Jesse. "I cannot imagine how hard this has been for you."

Tears began to well in Lucy's eyes, but she fought them back. "I'm doing okay, Jesse," she assured him. "How is it going with you and Beverly?"

"We're doing better than most, I suppose," Jesse reassured her. "We have been talking about getting married soon. We will have you and some others over for dinner when we get settled in enough to pull off a dinner party. We plan to make the formal announcement then."

"That's wonderful, Jesse. I am so happy for you. I mean that. John would've been delighted, too."

"I think we're all here," called Michael Wilson to the others. "Why don't we go in and get started?"

.   .   .   .   .

Upstairs, the Sanibel library was adorned by a rather lavish conference room with highly polished woodwork and a long table. Jesse sat at one end: Michael, at the other. The three women sat along one long side; Jeffrey, Barefoot Chuck, and Bert sat along the other long side. This counsel of eight men and women was charged with the repair and maintenance of Sanibel society. It was a tall order made more difficult by the vengeful plundering of General Alderman's seasoned mercenaries.

"Ladies, gentlemen," began Jesse. "Let's get started. We have a lot to do today with this first meeting. We need to begin taking an inventory, both of human resources and materials. We need to know what we have in terms of the basics: food, clothing, shelter; water, power, safety; medical needs, spiritual needs, communication, and transportation. We need to establish priorities, especially with regard to those items that we need and do not have; but also, we need to know what we're running out of. We need to establish either currency or a barter system, or some hybrid of both. We need to find a way to instill some confidence in the people that we are going to be alright, both in the short term and for years to come. In short we need to become self-sustaining, and we need to do it as a community that is in agreement with both our goals and our methods. I told you this was going to be a tall order, so let's get started."

"Well, I will go first because I know what my role needs to be," Barefoot Chuck spoke up. "I am the fisherman here. I have a few boats. I know where the fish are. I know who on the island knows how to fish, and who cannot find the end of the hook to put the worm on. I need to organize the island's fishing fleet."

"Perfect," agreed Jesse. "If you can add to that the responsibility of putting together some sort of market, where people can buy the fish from the fishermen, that would be the icing on the cake."

"Can do, Jesse," said Barefoot Chuck who was starting to scribble notes on a tablet and make a list of names of people he knew who could catch fish. "You know we're lucky we are as far south as we are. A little further north and throughout most of the Gulf coastline, it is a dead zone. There's not enough oxygen to support life. Fish that migrate through there get disoriented and die. It's not as large as the dead zones in the Pacific with its gyres of plastic trash, but it's big enough and it's growing."

"I thought that all happened decades ago," Bert spoke up, "With oil spills and chemical dispersants, flooding that washed fertilizer and pesticides into the Mississippi basin, and the overfishing that the new technologies gave us, but it seems to have a mind of its own now. The dead zone in the Gulf's bigger every year, but it hasn't reached us yet."

"Does that mean we have more fish crowded into our healthier waters?" asked Mercedes.

"I wish it did work like that, but we actually have less. It's not as if the fish escaped to our waters. They died in the dead zone and they are not coming back. Plus, many of the fish off our coast migrate. They swim into the toxic soup where there is no oxygen, and they don't make it back. But I don't want to make it too bleak sounding. Like I said before, we're lucky; we're fortunate to have a decent fish population in these waters. You pescatarians can rejoice."

"Pescatarians!" Jesse whistled. "You amaze me sometimes, Chuckles."

"Well, you have to expect an old fisherman to know his clientele," grinned Barefoot Chuck right back at the smiling Jesse. "The elitist folks on Sanibel enjoyed the word play."

Jesse kept it going. "While we are on the subject of food supplies, what do we know about what is left on the island that will tide us over until we can get some crops harvested?"

Lucy spoke first. "Some people are telling me they are hungry, but I'm not sure if supplies are running short or they just do not know where to look. I have food in my pantry but not enough to last me more than a month or two, and we're not receiving shipments like we used to."

Michael spoke next. "I have been in touch with several mainland suppliers of both food and medicine. They seem willing to work with us. They think we're a good bet to come through this and make them whole. There is still some gold on the island; Alderman's men didn't find it all. We should be able to replenish basic food stocks, but we better not depend on these suppliers' generosity for very long. We also should focus on nutritional value and not spend scarce resources on processed foods. I recommend that we focus on fruits, vegetables, beans, nuts, low-fat dairy, whole grains, fish, olive oil and a little wine. Anything else we simply don't need and can't afford right now. If we get started with the crops, we will soon have locally-grown organic plants to supplement or even supplant the mainland produce."

"That's actually better than I had hoped for, Michael. Your point about there still being some gold on the island is a good one. I am not sure how to go about levying some kind of tax or other assessment, and I'm not sure I would want to. The council will need some funds to work with, however, so I think initially what we might do is volunteer some funds – and by that I mean gold – out of our own pockets. I know Beverly and I have some that can go into a community fund. And if any of you can contribute, that's great. And we can ask for other donations from the community. I would consider it an investment in the survival and sustainability of the island." Jesse had scanned the others as he spoke, and through eye contact felt a reassurance that they were in agreement and would chip in according to their ability. "Now, on to another topic: what about security?"

"The town needs a sheriff," said Jeffrey, the former NSA agent.

"Are you volunteering?" Jesse asked. He already knew the answer.

"Yes," replied Jeffrey. "I can volunteer at least temporarily and maybe longer if it works out for everyone. I have a law enforcement background and some organizational skills. I can set up some community watch groups and try to enforce some commonsense behaviors. I really think that the way people on the island are coming together, that there really should not be much call for a sheriff to get involved. But you never know."

"Are you okay with Jeffrey being the new sheriff, Lucy?" Jesse said as he turned to the previous sheriff's widow.

"Of course I am, Jesse, but thanks for considering my feelings," replied Lucy. She turned to Jeffrey and added, "I have some of John's things, including the badge and other implements of the office. You are more than welcome to them, but I want to keep his service revolver. I am comfortable with it and I certainly know how to use it."

"Thanks, Lucy. I'll be by to get the badge and the other things later, if that's okay with you." Jeffrey looked at her and nodded. Lucy nodded back at him.

"So that is food and safety. Is there enough housing for everyone?" Jesse put the question to the group.

"I have not seen people sleeping in the streets," began Michael. "I also have not run across any homelessness in the patients that I have been seeing. I think that there were so many condo units on Sanibel, that even after all of the shelling and door to door shooting, everybody seems to have a place to stay. That's not a very scientific inventory, but I'll let you know if the picture changes. We may need to work on food distribution, but I think clothing and shelter are covered."

Jesse took the lead on the distribution point. "That's good, Michael, I agree. Lucy, I would like to assign you to creating a system of marketplaces and commerce, if that appeals to you. I was thinking that we could look at some of the old shopping plazas and convert them into something like flea markets so that people could trade out the things they don't want for the things they do need."

"That sounds right up my alley, Jesse," agreed Lucy. "I'll start right away."

"Bert," said Jesse.

"Yes, sir," snapped Bert.

"Bert, I would like you to be in charge of the islands infrastructure. I know you can already handle the reverse osmosis at Island Water, but we need a lot more right now. As I was biking over here, I was impressed by how pockmarked and cratered some of the streets are. I doubt that will be going back to automobile traffic anytime soon, but the holes are dangerous for bikers and pedestrians. My thought is that a shovel brigade could fill them in;

maybe plant some native species. It would give a lot of people something to do in a hurry. Another thought I had is that we could take some bombed out buildings and convert them to chicken houses; but I don't think we should be doing anything more than letting them breed and increase in numbers this year. If we start eating chickens and their eggs now, they will be gone before we know it. I expect that you will be busy with people bringing you this project and that. Bike repair comes to mind. Are you up for it?"

"Yes sir! Bring it on," said Bert brightly.

"Liz and Mercedes," said Jesse, focusing on the last two.

They gave him their attention, but waited to see what he had to offer before they spoke.

"This may not seem like it should be the highest priority, but I believe that it is. The people have been through hell. They are devastated spiritually and their morale is tenuous at best. If people cannot find the will, the courage, or the optimism to do what has to be done, our council meetings and donations of gold will be for nothing."

Jesse had their attention. "I would like you to do for the island what you do best. I need you two

36

to nourish people's creativity and their need for play and recreation. Think about that word. If ever we needed re-creation, it is now. Liz, I'm asking you to be our artistic director, and Mercedes, I would like you to be the island's social director. Liz, I was thinking you could have art classes, pottery workshops – which I think would be useful, and whatever else you think would help get people out of their funk. Mercedes…"

"Alison can help you with the art classes," Michael Wilson said to Liz, interrupting Jesse as he volunteered Alison's services.

"Mercedes," Jesse began again.

"Yes, Jesse. Social director. Got it."

"Yes, but more than that. I also want you to be in charge of landscaping and cleanup of the fallen trees. I was thinking maybe as part of being social director, you could organize people into projects that involve new garden plantings and beautification. We are going to need a lot of gardening activity as soon as possible. Your challenge is to make it fun. We need to make people want to pitch in and be part of the solution. Can you do that?"

"Yes, Jesse. I think I can," said Mercedes confidently. "We will have those golf courses turned into cornfields and tomato patches before you can..."

"And yoga classes," interrupted Jesse. "People need to heal from the inside out," he continued. "We need yoga classes."

"Oh, yes," agreed Liz.

"And tai chi," Jesse continued.

"Okay, okay. Social director/miracle worker. You got it. Anything else?" Mercedes asked, but she was serious. She would get people organized, and she wanted the other people at the table to understand that she was as confident and determined as they were.

The meeting continued for another hour as details were explored and plans were formulated. It was a good beginning and everybody left the Council meeting feeling uplifted and enthusiastic. They would instill the same can-do spirit on the others. Sanibel was beginning to heal.

They were beginning to conclude the meeting when somebody asked, "Where is Henry Farber?" They were referring to the mayor of Sanibel.

"I have not seen him lately," said Lucy. "Has anyone else seen or heard anything of him?"

"I haven't," replied Jesse. "I know that doesn't mean anything, but it's another good reason to take some informal kind of census. We need to know how many people are in our community, how many need clothing and feeding and shelter anyway. Lucy, can you assign some people to that?"

"Okay, Jesse," agreed Lucy. "I know some people who can work on that."

"Okay, good. If anybody does see Henry, tell them that we're meeting in the library at this time every week. It would be good to have his input." Jesse rose to leave.

The others followed suit. Wilson added, "So, same time next week?"

"Everybody take care," Jesse nodded to the group.

.   .   .   .   .

Jesse spent the next several days working on the chainsaw brigade. It was not just that he wanted to demonstrate the spirit of volunteerism and encourage others to do the same, but mostly he just wanted to get away from the mental tasks and work the body in a comfortable familiar manner. Beverly would find excuses to bring iced tea to the workers, partly because it flat out turned her on to see her man sweating shirtless in his Carhartt shorts and Timberland work boots.

The work details included rapidly cleaning up the fallen Australian pines and palm trees. Neatly stacked cords of firewood were appearing everywhere. The residents of Sanibel would not need to worry about staying warm if temperatures dipped into the 50s this winter, although it was unusual for Sanibel to reach such lows in the last decade. At least global warming had not affected the shoreline too much yet. When the arctic ice caps melted there was little effect on ocean levels because of Archimedes' principle: the weight of the ice caps raised ocean levels about the same as the later melted volume. It was the runoff from glacier melt and the expanded volume due to rising ocean temperatures that were the real problems. But, as in previous decades, that was a problem for another day.

· · · · ·

That evening, alone together, Jesse and Beverly snuggled like the lovers they were, on an over-sized chaise lounge on a patio overlooking their private garden space. Jesse stared up at the countless stars like he had done on countless evenings on board *Serenity*. Beverly nuzzled her face into his neck so that her soft breathing caught the scent of his hair. She was curled provocatively: a breast on his chest, a thigh on his groin, her breathing tickling and warming his neck. Yet they were both too content to take it further.

"I love you," came a whisper.

"I love you, too," came another.

"Let's get married."

"We already are."

"OK, but let's have a ceremony."

"OK, when?"

"Tomorrow."

"Let's have friends over first."

"OK, day after tomorrow."

"OK, or Sunday."

· · · · ·

Jeffrey Rogers, the former NSA operative, had found a vantage point to his liking. He watched a raccoon moving with stealth, not the usual waddle. She was hunting and wary. On a tiny tree stand, little more than a bicycle seat with a foot rest thirty feet up an Australian pine, Rogers was sensed by her but neither seen nor heard. Jeffrey had no agenda other than to be alone and in control. If he could gather secret knowledge about nocturnal comings and goings, it might come in useful someday.

A human approached along a bike path. Rogers watched in even greater silence. He moved imperceptibly to make himself even smaller. As the human approached, the raccoon disappeared into the bushes. The tree frogs grew noisier. The breeze faltered then grew again. She passed under the tiny hidden platform, unhurried but deliberate.

"Where is she going?" wondered Rogers. "Who else is out, and why?"

The questions were registered and cataloged, but they did not haunt him. He had no agenda other than to be alone and in control; and to someday exact vengeance.

January 18, 2025

Liz Forbes and Mercedes Phillips had put out the call. Their friends had contacted friends and the resultant gathering had outgrown the supply of prepared food and drink. Two mavens uniting social circles were a force with which to reckon.

They could not help but marvel at the change that had come over people. Where there was once selfish competition and mean-spirited betrayals, like some social game of who has the most, the best, the biggest, now there was caring and sharing and 'how can I help'.

Giving faith and hope a chance may not have been such a third rail as one might have thought. Science is based upon being able to repeat results, and on the most fundamental level, we know that

43

quantum probability is involved; and in perfect balance, there is faith in the divine. In fact, the whole of our understanding of God is a razor's edge, and just as dangerous.

Circles of friends developed where before there was indifference. People worked in the corn fields in groups of three or seven, talking earnestly about life and feelings and, importantly, hope for the future. The connections were continued in the evenings where new contacts were made, and old friendships were deepened.

Everyone was now planting vegetable gardens in sunny locations near their homes. The abandoned landscaping nurseries were soon emptied of their semitropical blooms and vegetation as the Forbes-Phillips brigade filled the potholes and scars – souvenirs of the recent shelling – turning Sanibel back toward the visual paradise of yesteryear. The beautification project went quickly with many willing hands. Deceptively it seemed like a superficial undertaking, but truly it was something much deeper, soul sustaining, and nourishing. It was tangible optimism – a belief in tomorrow.

.   .   .   .   .

Plans were also taking shape to harness alternate energy sources – wind, geothermal, solar and the tides. Work was begun for construction of a backup generator for the water pumping station powered by solar panels.

.   .   .   .   .

Jesse was a veritable trifecta of wealth. If a person is rich based on what he or she can do without – a true absence of desire for the material – then Jesse had long proved his worth aboard his sailing ship, *Serenity*. To the extent that wealth is based on friendships and relationships, the respect of others, the love and trust, then Jesse was the *de facto* king of Sanibel. As for gold, Beverly and Jesse have long debated their relative holdings. To be absolutely honest, neither knew for sure how much each had, but it was a lot. Beverly's fortune was inherited from Brady Chapman, Sanibel's orchid aficionado and international hit man. Jesse's suspected wealth was long thought to be from an inheritance, but in fact was derived from Software Innovations, a Silicon Valley startup company, and a billion-dollar buyout from an internet behemoth just prior to the crash of 2020. Timing is everything.

January 31, 2025

"Hello, is anybody home?" asked Liz as she walked through the front door.

"We're out back on the patio," called Beverly. "Come join us."

"Sorry I got here early." said Liz looking around the patio and gardens beyond. "What can I do to help?"

"It's all under control," replied Beverly. "Jesse has done most of the cooking."

"And it smells great."

"I know. Doesn't it? Are you ready for some bubbly?"

As if on cue, Jesse appeared from around the corner with a bottle in one hand and an assortment of champagne flutes hanging from the spaces between his fingers.

"Yes, please," said the women in unison, locking eyes and smiling.

"We'll have what you're having," added Beverly. "What do you have there?"

"This, dear ladies, is an Iron Horse Russian Cuvée. You will love it," declared Jesse as he slowly twisted and controlled the cork to keep it from popping. "Try it with the smoked fish and the grissini wrapped in prosciutto."

"Hello my lovelies. So glad you could make it," called Liz Forbes as Michael Wilson and Alison Swanson, engaged since the night of the attack on Sanibel, rounded the corner of the house.

"Greetings, doctor. You are looking radiant Alison," said Beverly as she filled their hands with appetizers and offered them the sparkling wine.

"Thanks," said Michael. "It's been a day!"

"Busy one?" asked Liz as she kissed his lips and lingered there.

"Indeed," replied the island's doctor. "We had our first chainsaw injury. It was just a matter of time. Went right through the shoe, but thankfully not the bone. But still, it was a bloody mess and just getting the boot off reminded me of how precious little morphine there is left. Wow, this is delicious."

"Oh, look, a squirrel!" laughed Liz at Michael's abrupt change in attention.

Others were beginning to file in: Barefoot Chuck, Bert Krepazhski, Mercedes Phillips and Lucy Cochran. The Council members attending made Jeffrey Rogers conspicuous by his absence.

Marti Leinhart, Sharon Welker, Thelma Coggins, Clyde Markowitz and a dozen others were finding their way into the setting and began helping themselves to the Russian Cuvée and smoked fish, fresh from the Gulf.

"Where is Antonio?" Beverly asked Marty.

"Tony has new interests," she replied. "I think he might've been too embarrassed to come with me."

"I'm sorry, Sweetie. I didn't know," said Beverly quietly as two friends found a quiet area away from the growing crowd.

As the crowd mingled and shifted, as old friends caught up on new concerns, and as bottles of the fragrant bubbly collected neck down in the

49

various ice buckets, the din and laughter rose to drown out the soft jazz coming from the patio speakers. Above all this a strong voice from the patio door proclaimed, "Come and get it!"

There was no table large enough to seat everyone so the dinner was served buffet style and the friends sat where they could find space. The first course was a favorite of Jesse's: cocoa crusted duck with peach sauce, polenta and crispy basil. The wine was a 2016 Rued zinfandel. This was followed by a bison Bolognese with mushroom ravioli and ricotta salata accompanied by a 2010 Heitz Cellars Cabernet Sauvignon. Brady Chapman continued to play the role of generous benefactor. His wine cellar, overlooked by Major Alderman's invaders, ran deep, rich and true. His walk-in freezer did as well. No one on Sanibel had seen such a feast in quite some time.

Almost no one spoke. There were murmurs of delight, but the flavors were hypnotic. Finally, Michael Wilson broke the trance.

"Jesse, where did you find these wines? And the meal is amazing. Whoever gave you the notion that you could cook a meal like this?"

"All in due time, Michael. Actually, this is not merely a random meal with friends. Beverly and I invited you all here to make a very special announcement. Actually two announcements," Jesse continued. He looked over at Beverly. She smiled at him sweetly.

"Beverly and I are getting married," he said with a flourish as the room burst into smiles and laughter. He looked around at their happy friends and saw Beverly, shaking her head slowly, imperceptibly, from side to side. Jesse then added softly, "actually, one announcement."

Everyone was standing now, laughing, hugging and kissing the bride to be, hugging and shaking hands with the groom to be. Dishes were being cleared and a palate cleansing dessert was finding its way onto small plates when there was a knock at the door. *Who knocks on Sanibel?*

Jesse opened the door to a forlorn looking Jeffrey Rogers. *I knew I should have invited Jeffrey,* thought Jesse. *I knew he would find out and would get his feelings hurt.* Too late now.

"Jeffrey, please come in," said Jesse warmly to the island's newly appointed sheriff.

51

"Another time, Jesse. Can you get Dr. Wilson and can the two of you come with me? I know it's late, but I could use some help. There's been a murder."

February 1, 2025

Time itself is finite, with a beginning and in 700 billion years, depending on what equation you use for the Hubble constant, an end. One can see the appeal, nevertheless, of religions that promise infinite life – world without end – amen. Buddhists offer enlightenment and becoming "awake", like the Buddha. Islamists offer a paradise with seven heavens, material delights, jewels and 72 virgin women. Hindus offer reincarnation. Mormans offer their men a planet. After death, the "Saints" —i.e., righteous Mormons—will become Gods with the ability to "frame" new worlds and will indeed have them to themselves, just as God has this one. The details are a bit murky.

The aging hippies at The Farm offered living in the present, life as usual, a sustainable tribe unchanged for over five decades. One can see the appeal of living in the present – vegetarians at one with the Earth. "Be Here Now" summarizes the mantra of many Eastern philosophies where living in the present effectively *mutes the angst* of having *finite* personal time.

In May, 2010, a 9.6 billion-year-old cluster of about 60 galaxies was seen and reported by separate teams of astronomers in Germany and Japan. The most distant galaxies are 12.8 billion light-years away. That means the light we see today was generated 12.8 billion years ago. Our universe is analogous to the flash of a lightning bug; it just lasts 700 billion years longer. Our portion of that – humans on Earth – is too tiny to assign a fraction to universal time.

Even our portion of Earth time is tiny, considering that the Earth is about 4.6 billion years old. The human occupation time on planet Earth is one one-hundred thousandth of a percent of Earth time and nevertheless, despite our brief time, we humans have had a significant impact on planet

Earth. And to our credit, the universe became aware of itself – sapient – when we did.

This then is the mindset at The Farm in the year 2025. This is where Jennifer Marin – beautiful and athletic Hispanic tennis pro – and Greg Johnston – conflicted but kind-hearted jack of all trades – find themselves in a situation. It may be time to leave. It cannot have been easy sustaining the tribes of an intentional community in Tennessee, based on principles of nonviolence and respect for the Earth. Stephen Gaskin and his 320 San Francisco hippy friends should be proud that their vision lasted as long as it did. No one could have predicted such a prolonged extreme drought in a temperate rain forest. Climate change aside, the novel coronavirus plus the economic collapse with pockets of starvation, food riots, and the toxic, sometimes violent, political divide, these forces brought down bigger societies than The Farm. Life that cannot adapt, spread and migrate will be among the increasingly extinct. At The Farm the root cellars became empty and spring planting was still months away. It seemed like a good time for Jennifer and Greg to move on – but to where?

．　　　．　　　．　　　．　　　．

It was after midnight when Jeffrey, Michael, and Jesse arrived at the crime scene. Jeffrey had cordoned off the area with the bright yellow police tape. His preliminary investigation had not turned up any clues in the moonlight. To his credit, he had not disturbed the body. She was a young fit woman who appeared to have been out for an evening's run.

Michael had stopped by his office to pick up some equipment. He removed a liver probe from his bag and deftly inserted it into the right upper quadrant of the victim's abdomen.

After a few minutes, Dr. Wilson looked up and pronounced, "33°C. Given the ambient temperature and a drop of 1.5°C per hour, and assuming that the victim was at 37.5°C and did not have a fever at the time of her murder, I can reasonably place the time of death at 9:30 PM. The degree of rigor mortis and the lividity all being in a dependent location are consistent with the estimated time of death, and suggest that the victim has not been moved. She was killed in this location. There are stab wounds to the vital organs that indicate that the killer knew exactly what he was doing. End of dictation."

"Can I get a copy of your report, doctor?" asked Jeffrey. "She did not have a wallet or any other form of identification on her, and I do not recognize her. Do either of you know her?"

"No, I don't. She isn't one of my patients. It will take a few days to complete a thorough forensic exam, Jeffrey. I will send you what I've got as soon as I know it. It looks like you got your first case, and it's a terrible way to begin your time as Sheriff."

"No kidding," Jeffrey agreed. "I honestly did not expect anything more than quarrels and quibbles. After all of the bloodshed of the invasion, I am not sure why the murder of one person should be so upsetting, but it is. Perhaps it is because she appears to be so young and vital, and the murder itself seems so brutal and senseless."

"I couldn't agree more," added Jesse. "This is just flat out sickening. I have tried policing the grounds, but I have not found any evidence to bag and tag. I'll come back at first light and try again, if that will be any help."

"Any help is greatly appreciated. I'll meet you here at daybreak and we can go over the area together. Meanwhile, let's load the body onto your Gator, Jesse, and take it over to Dr. Wilson's office. I will look for a cooler to serve as a makeshift morgue. Who would have thought we would ever need such a thing?"

"Just find the bastard," said Jesse. "I'm trying to figure out how to tell the women. This is going to be terribly upsetting to everybody on the island. The recovery effort has been remarkably full of cooperation until now. I am afraid of what this will do to the optimism and good spirits that everyone has worked so hard to achieve. Let's just hope for the best."

.   .   .   .   .

When Jesse arrived back home, the dinner party had dispersed. Marti and Beverly were bookends on the couch, each with their feet tucked under them, talking softly and sipping an herbal tea.

Beverly looked up at Jesse, "Was it bad?"

"Yes. A young woman jogger. Stab wounds from an attack earlier tonight. That's about all we know right now."

"Oh, Jesse. That is so terrible. I feel horrible and I have no idea what to think about it. Life just seems like it is on a roller coaster right now. Are you okay?"

"I am shaken, but okay. I need to get up before dawn and help Jeffrey look more closely around the crime scene when there is better light. I should get a few hours' sleep," he said then looked at Marti. "Thanks for keeping Beverly company tonight, Marti. I know she was happy to have some time with you."

"She knows our secret, Jesse," Beverly confessed.

"Announcement number two?" smiled Jesse.

"Well, it was not a difficult deduction," said Marti. "Beverly did not have so much as a sip of wine this evening. There is only one reason for a sacrifice so drastic. You guys are pregnant!"

"Indeed, we are," said Jesse, smiling. "Indeed, we are." And with that he kissed the ladies good night and headed to the bedroom for a few hours.

. . . . .

59

After a futile search of the crime scene at daylight, Jeffrey and Jesse found their way to Dr. Wilson's office. The office was nicely furnished with colorful leather wingback chairs and Oriental carpets, rich wood wainscoting and contemporary art on the walls. It felt welcoming, like someone's home, rather than being clinical or sterile.

They found Dr. Wilson in the back, examining the woman's body on a stretcher that served as a makeshift morgue slab. As the two approached, Dr. Wilson straightened a flexible probe and inserted it into one of the chest wounds.

"Look at this," said Dr. Wilson. "This has developed into a very interesting case. Do we have a name yet?"

"Not yet," replied Jeffrey. "I have digital photos to share and I am sure she has friends on the island who will recognize her, if not report her missing soon. The grassy area near where she had been running had nothing more than the usual trash. We bagged everything so some community clean-up got done if nothing else."

"Well, come look at this," suggested Dr. Wilson. As they gathered close to the body, he continued. "The probe over the heart meets resistance at six inches. So does this one that penetrated the lung, and this one, and this one over the liver. And look at the ecchymoses around each wound. I am no medical examiner, but that strikes me as unusual. These jagged areas are on just the one side but not the other. That suggests a military knife with a serrated edge, six inches long and thrust to the hilt every time and with such force as to compound each wound with bruising from the impact. Whoever did this is vicious, out of control and seething with anger. We may have some sort of psychopath in our midst.

"That is very helpful, doctor," said Sheriff Rogers. "The knife especially does not sound like a common item, although it could have been left behind by Alderman's troops, and anybody could have found it."

"True," added Jesse, "but not just anyone could have the skills to kill that methodically."

"There's more," Wilson chimed in. "He, and I say 'he' because of the brute force. He went for the heart first. The heart wound bled but also would have caused arrhythmia and cardiac arrest. The other wounds have much less bleeding because the heart would have already stopped pumping. The other wounds were gratuitous, merely angry stabbing. There were no defensive wounds, nothing under the fingernails either."

"Very thorough, Sir," Jeffrey Rogers complemented Wilson obsequiously. "We have some things to go on now. Please send me a report when you get finished. I will start asking questions and showing her picture around. Something will turn up, I'm sure."

"Good hunting," said Jesse. "Call me if you discover any new evidence, or if I can help."

"Will do."

.   .   .   .   .

The accumulated gold from the island's principals was used to start the Bank of Sanibel. No one showed any interest in making the name of the bank sound too clever. Deposits and loans were made, and script was handwritten by the bank's officers, those who had deposited and provided physical gold. Soon even those residents of Sanibel Island who had been left with no funds and no material resources were able to purchase from the ever-accumulating food supplies.

There were so many Monopoly game boards among the thousands of island condos, that someone had the jolly idea of using the Monopoly money as legal Sanibel tender. All someone needed to do was issue a promissory note to the bank – "I promise to work to pay this back." – then the bank officer would initial the Monopoly money, making it legal. It was a splendid affectation. Island residents could not help but grin and chuckle as they paid for bartered goods or services.

.   .   .   .   .

February 6, 2025

Beverly began her day searching for Jesse. The task was made easier by knowing his routines. The task was made more difficult by the physical layout of the house itself and the gardens. The house they inherited from Brady Chapman was 40 years old and a sprawling structure with many sections, nearly 5000 square feet not counting the greenhouse. It was still decorated with many of Chapman's furnishings and pieces of artwork. Brady clearly had had excellent taste. As a top-tier assassin he could afford the best, and over three acres of sandy loam on the once exclusive island certainly qualified as the best.

Beverly made her way outside. She used to be the early riser, but that changed early in her pregnancy. Still no Jesse. The Lightspeed was leaning against the house at the far end of the patio, so she kept looking. Beyond the gardens in the trees to the West, she found him sitting in a half lotus position on a blanket of pine needles, meditating. He was focused but not in a trance, so as she approached, he smiled broadly and rose to greet her. They embrace tenderly and long.

"Do you want some breakfast?" he asked.

"How about if we go for a walk?"

"How about if we go for a bike ride?"

"Okay. Let's," she agreed.

They wheeled onto Beach Drive, turned right onto East Gulf with the sun at their backs, and pedaled at a moderate pace, watching cautiously for potholes. The scars of the shelling were daily reminders of the assault on Sanibel from Alderman's forces. The beautification effort to plant native vegetation in the larger potholes had begun on Periwinkle but had not yet spread to other roads. While excellent for strolling and biking, someone had pointed out that car traffic in the future would not be possible. Jesse had smiled at him and nodded as if to say that that was the whole idea. Jesse was all about the carbon footprint. Another reason to fill the

65

potholes was to eliminate many sources of standing water that would serve to breed mosquitoes. Spraying the island with chemicals to kill the larvae was no longer an available option. Historically, when left to its own natural proclivity, Sanibel bred mosquitoes abundantly.

Jesse and Beverly stopped frequently to talk with people working in their yards or walking along the sidewalks. The only thing that the people seemed interested in talking about was the murder of the young woman. Had Sheriff Rogers made any progress? Do we know yet who she was? Jesse said he did not know any more than anyone else at this point. Everyone looked concerned, and it was clear the early optimism was fading. There was a lot of work to do, much of it physical labor, and in a way that was for the best. It helped to keep people's minds off the realities of the larger struggle ahead when they had to stay focused on the day's task at hand.

Turning left onto Nerita, Beverly suggested that they stop at Sharon Welker's condo. They hadn't seen their old friend in weeks. They had been making it a point to keep a close eye on Sharon since that time last year when they discovered her near death and in despair.

That visit in 2024 was tragic. It took some time for Sharon to respond to their knock on the door, but after an interval the door opened warily to reveal a gaunt and bleary-eyed woman, still in her bathrobe. Sharon was having more than a bad hair day.

"I'm glad to see you two," Sharon said weakly as she forced a smile. Sharon spoke softly, sadly, subdued. Her speech was not slurred but Beverly and Jesse could smell alcohol, and as they paraded past the kitchenette toward the living room, they could see bottles in the trash.

They were all quiet for a moment then Jesse spoke sympathetically. "It's not fun anymore is it?"

"No, Jesse, it is definitely not fun," agreed Sharon.

"What can we do to help?" asked Beverly.

"Stay for a bit," replied Sharon. "I don't get a lot of company, well actually not any. Tell me what's going on. Is the fighting over? Have those horrible men gone? They raped me. I'm 53 years old, and they gang raped me like I was being punished for the sins of others. They tied me down when they left. The only food or water that I got was when they came back, until one day they didn't come back. I thought they had gotten tired of the 'old woman', or maybe they had gotten killed. I got to a place where it was now or never. My feet were free but my wrists were tied to the bedposts with lengths of rope. Listen to me. I got my feet under me, then behind my back against the headboard. Can you picture this? I was on my knees then and I walked backwards on my knees, feet going up the headboard, face going down to the mattress and arms stretched so tight I thought my shoulders would pop out. Then I squirmed and struggled to get my knees up on top of the headboard. Holding the ropes in both hands, I pushed the wall with my feet and the bed slid forward. The rest was easy. With my stomach on the top of the headboard, I dropped my feet to the floor and started pushing the bed. I made it as far as the dresser where there was a whisky bottle. I broke it and cut the rope with the broken glass. The next whiskey bottle I found, I just sat down and drank it. All of it." The narrative she told of those darkest of times haunted their memories even now.

They recalled how Sharon began to cry. She looked to Beverly as if she had aged a decade. She looked tired, moved slowly, and had the weariness of defeat on her.

"Oh, honey, I had no idea," Beverly had said.

"No, Beverly. There is no way you could have known. But answer me this first: are they gone? Or are they occupying Sanibel still?"

"They are gone, Sharon. They left. They took as many valuables as you can stuff into a convoy of 18 wheelers. Still there is a lot more left than anyone thought there would be. There is more than enough to feed us for the time being." People had forgotten that Sanibel was about the same size as Manhattan, roughly 12 miles long and 3 miles wide. The golf courses could be made into fertile farmland, Jesse had reassured her.

Sharon broke down sobbing that day until she could not get her breath. "Thank God if it's really over."

"It's over, honey. Believe it," said Beverly.

Sharon's face was pained, her lower jaw trembled so badly she could barely make the words come out. "I've only been away from these walls a few times, and only at night, running from one hiding place to the next, breaking into abandoned condos looking for food and booze."

"It's funny," she smiled wryly. "The liquor that people leave behind in their condos is usually the good stuff, expensive brands, and it's always hidden in the same location – that one cabinet, the "owners" cabinet, with the stainless steel lock that says "here's where the booze is.""

"What about it?" Jesse had asked. "How much are you drinking and are you getting enough to eat?"

"Don't judge me, Jesse. I am both stronger and more fragile than you can imagine. The brutality was not my first rodeo. I had my share of depression and what they used to call PTSD during and after the food riot years. I am better already now just knowing that they are gone. I ran out of the last of the alcohol – schnapps, if you can believe – two weeks ago. The withdrawal was pretty bad, but I've been through worse. The food's gone too. If you're hungry, I can offer you some ketchup packages.

"Get dressed and come with us," insisted Jesse. "The local restaurants have been set up as community kitchens. Volunteers are cooking homestyle meals, and there is enough to go around."

"I don't know if I can, Jesse. I'm a little weak and shaky."

"Get dressed, honey," said Beverly reassuringly. "All you have to do is sit on the bike and hold on to our shoulders. Rest your feet on the pedals and we will do the pushing. The fresh air and sunshine will do you good."

"Not to mention a real meal," Sharon agreed with a smile sweeter than before.

Jesse and Beverly had rolled her down Nerita drive as a red-shouldered hawk cried its familiar cry: "*Keeyer...keeyer...keeyer...keeyer*." The sun shone as if for the first time. The breeze blew in an attempt to dry the tangled but freshly washed hair. The beachcomber needed a beautician. But first a decent meal, and a check-up.

In his mind Jesse pictured a creature emerging from years in a cave to a sun bright world, welcome but painful, as least for the time being.

"Give Sharon your sunglasses," he suggested enigmatically to Beverly.

"Here. I have an extra pair," offered Beverly, digging in her bike pack behind her seat.

Only recently sober, Sharon was already feeling better from the attention and the activity.

71

Beverly and Jesse were still pushing Beverly's bicycle on which Sharon was seated. They had passed by new construction of some industrial size greenhouses and it gave Beverly the idea that she should crowd Brady's orchids to one end to make room for starting vegetables.

They turned left onto Periwinkle when the trio spotted Alison and fixed her in their collective gaze. Once she returned their gaze, she immediately started running toward them.

"Sharon," she cried. "Thank God you're not dead. Or are you?"

"Not yet," Sharon replied. "But damn near. If Beverly and Jesse had not come by, I'm not sure what would have happened to me. I've been too numb to care."

"You better see Michael," advised Alison, referring to her fiancé and the island's general practitioner.

"Not until after we get her something to eat," said Jesse. "Is the Jacaranda open yet?"

"It should be," replied Allison. "I saw some of the volunteers going that way earlier."

Several minutes later the four friends entered the sprawling restaurant that had been repurposed as a community kitchen. They were shown to the buffet and began dishing fresh local fish and vegetables on their plates. Sharon kept her portions small as she was not used to eating "regular food", and it seemed wise to test the waters, so to speak.

There was not much discussion about Sanibel or what had been going on in the last few months. There would be plenty of time for Sharon to catch up. Now was the time for comfort, support, reassurance, and friendship. Now was the time for healing. Allison had not yet heard about the rapes, and even Jesse and Beverly did not yet know how repetitive they had been. Sharon was starting to feel better in the quiet supportive company of her friends.

Today was quite different from that low point a year ago. Sharon beamed at them as she opened the door to their knock. "I hear you two are expecting", she said as a greeting.

.   .   .   .   .

Sheriff Rogers was maneuvering the flatboat among the mangrove forest at the edge of Tarpon Bay. He was looking for people he did not know and had not met yet. He was still searching for the identity of the deceased young woman.

In each encounter he would describe the woman and, if necessary, show a digital picture of her features in death. It was not a pleasant picture, nor was it flattering. Many found it repulsive and turned their heads quickly away.

Rogers tried to avoid dawn and dusk. Even in winter the mosquitoes were busier at these times when the wind was still. He also tried to avoid periods of heavy rain, but pop-up showers on Sanibel were inevitable and simply went with the job.

As Jeffrey Rogers motored quietly through the waters along the edge of the bay, he tried to piece together the scant clues he did have. The victim was a woman in her mid-20s, an amateur athlete, attractive but not beautiful, and not so much as a name or a social context. The perpetrator was a complete unknown. He was presumed to be male due to the brute force involved in the attack. The viciousness could have been driven by anger or insanity. It appeared that he came upon the woman from behind – not an easy task considering that she was herself already running at a moderate jogger's pace. The killer himself was athletic and obviously stayed in shape. The first contact, Jeffrey knew, would have been a strong left hand over her mouth and nose to squelch any attempt to scream, followed by a jerk back towards his body that stopped her in her tracks and threw her backwards and off-balance against him. At least that's how Jeffrey would have done it based on his military training.

The second move, a second or two later, would have been an upper thrust of the six-inch blade just below the xiphoid process and into the right ventricle of the heart. Such a blow would serve to lift her off her feet and would bring death rather quickly. There was no forensic evidence of the struggle, so that fit the evidence that they did have. What made no sense were the multiple other stab wounds. The killer was one angry sick dude.

Jeffrey brooded over these details as he slowly motored the small boat as far into the mangrove forest as it would take him. He was about to turn around when he spotted a ramshackle construction site. He tied the flat bottom boat to a tree and approached the shacks on foot. He was impressed by the construction skills. Someone or several someones had confiscated and repurposed doors, windows, and other debris from the invasion and shelling to create shelters hidden deep in the forest.

He called out, "Hello, I'm Jeffrey Rogers. I'm the new Sheriff. Is anybody home?"

A man stepped out from the nearest shack. He was unarmed. "Hello yourself," he replied. "How can I help you, Sheriff?"

"We found a woman's body, and I'm trying to identify her. Do you mind taking a look at her picture?"

"Let me see it." The man limped slowly toward the Sheriff. He was a large man and muscular, possibly one of the mercenaries from Island Security, and probably injured during the battle of Sanibel. "My name's Russell McGee, by the way. I am what's left of the troops that were stationed here."

Russell looked at the photograph on the Sheriff's cell phone. His eyes slowly started to swell with tears. "Yes, I know her. Knew her." Russell

76

thrust the phone back to Sheriff Rogers. He had seen too much.

"What can you tell me about her?" asked the sheriff.

"She was a secretary, administrative assistant, in our Sundial headquarters. Her name is, was, Jamie Siskind. Everybody called her "Sissy", both because of her last name and because she was like everybody's sister. We left during the worst of the bombardment. I guess I was a deserter but it wasn't because I was afraid to die. Hell I wish I had died. No it was just that I was trying to get Sissy to safety. We made it here to the mangroves and dug in. I was wounded as you can see, and she nursed me back to where I could get around some. She would go out after dark and look for stuff that we could use, mostly food and shelter. She sure did not deserve this. What happened? Who did this to her? Was it that bunch that invaded us? Are we still occupied?"

"No, they pulled out in December a year ago after helping themselves to anything and everything of value. No, we don't have a clue as to who did this to Ms. Siskind. I am kind of a police force of one, and new at it. Come to think of it I could use a deputy with your background. Would you be interested?"

"Man, that is tempting," said Russell. "I am barely surviving out here. But I cannot even begin to process that. Sissy was more than a sister/friend these last few months. We had each other and we still had our lives, and that was it. You know? It is going take me some time to get over her. You know, I had decided that she had gone out for one of her runs, met someone, and decided simply to leave me behind. The only thing even remotely positive about her murder is knowing that she had not run out on me. She hadn't rejected me, although I could not blame her if she had. It's pretty rugged sitting out here in the mangroves."

Russell paused. Sheriff Rogers maintained a respectful silence. "On the other hand," continued Russell, "I have no future hiding out in the forest indefinitely. If there is anything I would be motivated to do in this miserable life, it is to find Sissy's killer. Sheriff Rogers, I accept your offer. Deputize me. Let's get that bastard."

"Let's get the bastard," echoed Jeffrey. "Come with me Russell. Let's find you a vacated condo and a good meal."

.   .   .   .   .

Jeffrey told Russell that his return to polite society was reminiscent of Sharon Welker's return. Russell appreciated the story as Jeffrey Rogers related it. It made him feel less alone and made Sanibel sound welcoming and humanizing. It did not, however, help Russell forget his role, *his MOAS*, in the slaughter of civilians at the Caloosahatchee massacre.

Sheriff Rogers came through the door of the Jacaranda with the man from the mangrove forest, waking Russell from his musings. He nodded toward Jesse and the three women at his table, but did not speak as the two made their way toward the buffet line that had been steadily growing. When their turn finally came, McGee filled his plate with generous portions until he risked the embarrassment of dropping precious food on the floor.

They sat at the table next to Jesse and his posse of women. Rogers introduced Russell McGee as his new deputy. Russell looked and smelled more

79

like an escaped prisoner, but the others smiled politely as Jeffrey explained Russell's military background, leaving out the parts about the dishonorable discharge and the mercenary stent with Island Security. *Need to know*, thought Rogers. *He's good*, thought McGee appreciatively.

"Girl's name was Jamie Siskin. Went by 'Sissy'," Rogers shared to show the progress he had made. "She was an administrative assistant at Island Security's headquarters over at the Sundial. She and Russell were holed up in the mangroves near Tarpon Bay."

And with *that* the lights went out, dimming the restaurant and threatening vital functions all over the island, as it turned out, including the frozen food supply.

"Now what?" said Alison.

"We paid the mainlanders as we always do," said Jesse. "They said that next time it would be more, but it's not time for the next payment yet."

"Time to get the generators up and running," said Jeffrey, getting up from his uneaten lunch plate.

Russell looked up anxiously, and Jeffrey sensed his conflict. "I've got this, Russell," said Jeffrey. "You finish eating. Get a shower at the station and put on a spare uniform. Find me later if you can. I'm not sure where I'll be. We'll work out other details later." And with that Sheriff Rogers was out the door.

"I'm going home to get *our* generator going. We have a freezer full of food that should not go to waste," said Jesse.

Deputy McGee called over from the adjacent table, "Can anyone tell me where 'the station' is located?"

February 9, 2025

The people of Sanibel were shocked and increasingly preoccupied by the murder as word spread. Some people volunteered information to Sheriff Rogers and Deputy McGee concerning a "mysterious stranger" that lurked in dark places – several claimed to have seen glimpses, but their descriptions were variable and unreliable.

There was a grave side service for the murder victim held on the first Sunday afternoon after Sheriff Rogers released the body. It had been delayed for forensic reasons. The person who knew her best, her ex-lover Deputy Russell McGee, delivered a surprisingly eloquent eulogy.

It is difficult, to say the least, to try to make sense of the events that life throws your way. I happily surrender to God the issue of "Why". But still, one strives for closure. One wishes to understand how events unfold in a particular manner. One wishes to establish one's place among humanity, and from that reference point, one hopes to establish a value-driven purpose and meaning to one's existence.

I find myself looking for relief in expressions of God's grace – divine action that starts or stops cancer, creates or prevents floods, takes and gives life. Grace is an unexpected gift. Grace is free. It is not earned. The absence of grace is not a statement of moral depravity or anything moral at all. The experience of grace is not a statement about righteousness. Anything free, loving, and kind is grace. And it is abundant. One's life is one such gift, and the loss of the life of someone close is another. By losing something so precious, we can appreciate our loved ones, family and close friends, ever so much more keenly.

Grace takes us by surprise. It comes in odd packaging. It sometimes looks like loss, or failures. It's both reliable and unpredictable. It is not often what you are aiming for, but it supplies what you need, even if it is not necessarily what you want. It grows you up. It reminds you with a jolt that you are not in control, and not being in control is a form of freedom.

Our lives are a gift of grace. As for me, I shall always treasure the memories of Jamie Siskin. I know that I am better for having known her. I know that I carry a part of Sissy with me. If I can be a kinder friend, a better person, then perhaps my life, well lived, can be part of her legacy.

To the extent that we maximize our relationship with others, welcome the stranger, practice the art of hospitality in whatever way we can, as has been the case for me by you here on Sanibel; by doing these things, we transform the world.

The islanders were becoming distrustful and paranoid. Russell's words were a needed inspiration and were clearly heartfelt. He made the stranger *real* to each of the two hundred or so mourners attending the funeral.

84

. . . . .

Even Beverly herself sensed that she was being watched if not stalked. Jesse spent the night standing guard over the homestead for several nights after Beverly dreamed that she escaped a knife attack. After it began to show that Jesse was needing more sleep than he was permitting himself, Beverly started insisting that he should come to bed when she did.

"It was just a dream," she said, appealing to his rational side.

"I know," he responded wearily. "Still..."

They were cuddled on the sofa when Beverly asked Jesse about what he thought of the wisdom of bringing a child into a troubled world.

"We will just have to make it less troubled," Jesse said after a lengthy reflection.

As usual, Jesse kept his deeper thoughts to himself. It's daunting to talk to knowledgeable, insightful people who are so sure things are going to fall apart, and also sure that a little better version of the same old thing won't be enough. Jesse was offering a realistic promise that out of this crisis, we will find resilience. We will be reliant on ourselves and our communities and that is what counts. That's the way of nature, including human nature.

His meditations over the years had instilled in him the core Buddhist principle of interdependence, the teaching that there are no self-sustaining, permanent, inherently existing entities; that everything emerges as part of a great web of life and its interlocking relationships. In Buddhism, however, the understanding of interdependence is coupled with the practical understanding of the mind discipline necessary to break the habit of treating entities as permanent and independent. To get us out of our mess requires more than an intellectual understanding of what's wrong and what's right with civilization and its worship of the material.

Mindfulness – awareness meditation – allowed Jesse to quell the anxious roiling of the mind and to *focus* so intently that the mind could not be distracted and stressed by "what if" scenarios or by useless worried reminiscences. Jesse could see the world optimistically, and those in it in all of their splendor. Frankly, it was hard for him to conceive of how we can genuinely change our world view and way of acting without such a discipline, but he knew the discipline would have to find the individuals. Jesse could not bestow the gift of searching. Without it, however, in the face of chaos, uncertainty, and fear, Jesse knew that we "killer apes" would fall back into fighting for dominion over what we imagine to be "our world".

As for the issue of bringing a child into a deeply troubled world, it was the ultimate expression of optimism. To plant a garden is to believe in tomorrow, as Audrey Hepburn once said. Regardless of how deeply ingrained our self-defeating habits are, human beings know what they want at bottom, even if there is not complete agreement on how to achieve the end result. One thing we all agree on is that we care about our kids. We want the best possible future for them and we have a pretty clear conception of what that good future means. It's not a future full of material stuff, but a future in which our children are secure and safe and can develop their potential and flourish as human beings. Jesse was all about bringing their child into the world.

Jeffrey Rogers left work earlier, went home and took a nap. That night while the island mostly slept, he found himself in a familiar situation – up high in an Australian pine, sitting on a deer stand and watching for human goings and comings. The patterns and nocturnal habits were what interested him. It was, as before, the stealth and solitude, the sense of control and mastery, that appealed to his restless spirit. He did feel calmer than before, but not calm enough. There was very little activity tonight – one couple walking home perhaps after an evening with friends – but by and large, people were staying inside. They were spooked by the murder. Who could blame them? It seemed so brutal and random.

After a while Jeffrey's thoughts seethed with the smoldering, festering anger that he harbored toward his so-called friends, especially Jesse and Beverly. He had always admired Beverly as a fine-looking woman, but she had never returned his glances and overtures in any meaningful ways, merely the polite dismissal. *Dismissals!* It might seem irrational to some, but Jeffrey blamed Jesse for the egregious betrayal at the Mad Hatter just before the Battle of Sanibel. *I wouldn't be surprised if Jesse was responsible for Sanibel's downfall,* thought Jeffrey, making the association. *He did sail away like the coward that he is that very same night. He probably brought the invaders here, arranged everything. Just look at him now – large and in charge. We used to be poker buddies, but now nobody wants to be MY friend. Nobody. And for what? I made some money selling weapons in Africa. What is the big deal, really?* The soliloquy ran through Jeffrey's thoughts tonight like it did most nights. Sometimes his thoughts raced and splintered. The only thing that could get them quiet for a while was some cathartic distraction. *A judgment day is coming, but I may be wrong. You see I hear these funny voices...* he hummed the lyrics to an old song.

Jeffrey was smart. Every relationship was a chess game to be analyzed. He had the need to stay several steps ahead of everyone in his life now. No one could be trusted. Every single person he knew had the potential for betrayal. No one, not a single soul, not even his mother, especially his mother, had seemed to be there for him.

With Jesse the game was simple. To begin with, Jesse does not even know there is a game, doesn't at all recognize that there is a risk to him or Beverly or anyone. *Not a clue.* Jeffrey's strategy of befriending him and praising his leadership gratuitously in public was paying off. Jesse said to several people how Jeffrey had matured and was pitching in for the betterment of all, and what a remarkable change this represented. Those kind words got back to Jeffrey as you would expect in a small interdependent community. People were generally optimistic. There was hope for the island after all, and Jeffrey played a big role in that.

February 28, 2025

"Marry me," Beverly called to Jesse as he got out of bed.

Surprised, he turned back to look at her. "Well, yes. I think that is happening... going to happen... very high level of certainty... What are you talking about?"

"I know you asked me last month, but today I get to ask you. It's Sadie Hawkins day, so I am asking *you*. Will you marry me?"

"There's no leap day this year. You will need to wait until 2028 for the next Sadie Hawkins day."

"Capp never specified February 29th," Beverly came back.

"Okay then, I accept, my lady."

Beverly got up also. Her morning sleepy-head routine was fading, and her morning nausea was completely gone. She went to the closet and flipped the light switch. Nothing. She tried a few other electrical sources and they were just as unresponsive.

Electricity was becoming undependable with periodic outages, despite Jesse and Beverly paying the mainlanders from their own offshore accounts. Resentment from the massacre by out-of-control Island Security forces had resurfaced. It was much more than an inconvenience; it was a matter of survival. Irrigation of crops was jeopardized when the water supply, dependent on electricity, was cut off too often. Hardships become untenable to many of Sanibel's colonists. They had transitioned from a world of privilege and plenty to one of privation and productivity, but the unreliability of a basic, to them, necessity like electricity reminded them of their tenuous status and their vulnerability to outside forces. As the man says, "Sounds like a first-world problem to me."

Something needed to happen to fix the political power play. Jesse realized that he would have to travel to the mainlanders' headquarters in Fort Myers and negotiate an agreement. This was not a trip he was relishing. The journey would be risky for him, but moreover he would not be home to watch over Beverly. That was what really furrowed his brow.

·   ·   ·   ·   ·

Sheriff Rogers arrived at the station later than usual and Deputy McGee was already back from a morning patrol.

"Fresh pot of coffee," McGee offered.

"Thanks," replied Rogers, and he helped himself to some hot, black caffeine. "Anything of interest?"

"No, sir," Russell responded.

The murder investigation had gone cold and no one expected much new information after these last few weeks revealed nothing additional. There were no clues, no witnesses, and only one person who even knew the victim, and he was the deputy investigating the crime. Only time would tell if anything else would be revealed.

"There is a piece of unexploded ordinance in Doc Wilson's old neighborhood. That area was hit pretty hard for some reason. I don't think anyone lives there now, but I want you to check it out and see if the shell can be neutralized. Do you have any training in ordinance?" asked Jeffrey.

"Not much," replied the deputy. "Just what was in the manuals and that just covered the basics."

"That's still more than I know," admitted the former NSA operative. "Check it out and see what can be done. OK?"

"Yes, sir."

Jeffrey liked the young man's military bearing and routines. The station was maintained impeccably and stocked as if by a quarter master, everything they needed and nothing they did not.

Russell had been the attaché for one of the high-ranking officers in Island Security, the paramilitary force that was paid handsomely only a year-and-a-half ago to patrol and defend Sanibel. They employed the latest technology, including geosynchronous satellite imaging. In the end, however, Alderman's Army of the Association was the irresistible force, and they swept Sanibel clean.

Russell himself, unlike the organization he served, was moral. He did the right thing whenever it was not a direct violation of orders. He was loyal, however, and it was a soldier's duty to die. Everybody understood that. The exception in Russell's case was after the officers were dead and the force was destroyed, and there was a civilian – "Sissy" Siskin – to get to safety. Russell was still loyal. It was just that he could shift allegiances from an entity that was no more, to one that needed him. Other attributes – competence, organizational skills, creativity, and attention to detail — were why Lieutenant Russell McGee was rapidly ascending the proverbial ladder within Island Security. Bottom line: McGee was a decent man. That he had skills was bonus material.

.   .   .   .   .

At The Farm, the day was warmer than most of the preceding February. The sun shone brightly but the mood was gloomy at the collective. Provisions were running low. Rationing was in its second year because of weather that brought tornadoes, flooding, and periods of drought. Crops had not failed entirely but "global weirding" had taken its toll. The aging hippies were used to hardships and roughing it, but reserves of physical strength were waning, endurance was waning. Optimism had run up against the realities of attrition, much like the local Baptist church whose younger members no longer came or contributed.

The real force behind The Farm was and always had been Stephen F. Gaskin, a professed "hippie priest and freelance rebel rouser" who assembled, preached to, and presided over The Farm, one of the largest and longest-lasting communes born of the counterculture era. When he died July 1, 2014, at 79, the *force* was dimmed irreversibly. Add the aging of the commune, the entropy of decaying structures and constant repair demands, and the infernal weather and pestilence, and the downward spiral was gaining momentum.

Douglas Stevenson tried his best to revive the idealism and organization. New people did come and stay for a while, like Jennifer, Fernando, and Greg, but they would stay only long enough to get their head straight, then move on. Gaskin was a countercultural celebrity, the figurehead of a commune that seemed to have achieved the critical mass, wherewithal and collective commitment needed to make such a society work when so many others had not. He was irreplaceable.

At the "campfire" that evening, someone was strumming a guitar and singing a song he had written three decades ago, titled *Fade*. It was written by Aaron Gabriel with sentiments and insights well beyond those expected of a tender youth, but tonight especially, it transferred the thoughts and feelings of the smallish tribe anthropomorphically to The Farm.

Aaron sang softly and with a poignant sadness. It was the quietest of gatherings, and among the most thoughtful.

It's never easy:
Watching the slow fade,
Watching the snow days
Melt into years.
It's never easy:
Letting go of the sun,
Putting your head back
And starting to run.
So you walk with the others
Like Churchill advised.

You put on your make-up
And stop taking sides.
And you bring out the old days,
And you serve 'em with beer –
Another book on the campfire,
Another night without fear.

And your Revolution:
You never found the time.
Yeah, you learned all the right words:
You never got them to rhyme.
You could have been a singer.
You could have carried the world.
You could have taken it all back.
You could have left with the girl.
And she would have told fortunes
With one look from her eyes.
Yeah we all could have ridden
Into hell at your side.
But no one fights forever;
No one fights alone.
Just another day older.
Just another step home.

Yeah we all could have ridden
Into hell at your side...
Into hell at your side.

You could have been a singer.
You could have carried the world.
You could have taken it all back.
You could have left with the girl.
No one fights forever;
No one fights alone.
Just another day older.
Just another step home.

March 13, 2025

March offered good news and bad. Jesse saved himself from risking a trip to Fort Myers by increasing the bank credits to the regional division of the Army of the Association by an exorbitant twenty-five percent. He negotiated through the bank officers at his bank on Grand Cayman. He was pleased to not become a known entity to an army of potential hotheads. There had been no further power outages for the last month.

The bad news, and it was really bad, was that Sanibel now had a pattern of murders. All were knife attacks: two were along trails, and two were as a result of home invasions. The first were two weeks apart, then ten days, and the most recent murder was one week after the one before it. The serial killer was needing his "fixes" more frequently. Whatever demons the bloodshed *had been* keeping at bay, the vicious catharsis was becoming progressively less effective.

In every case Sheriff Rogers, Deputy McGee, Doctor Wilson, and Jesse O'Connell investigated as a team. In every case the forensic evidence revealed consistent patterns of the knife wounds, never any defensive indications, no DNA, and no evidence at the crime scenes. They were the cleanest random killings any of the team had ever seen. After gathering what evidence they could find, Sheriff Rogers and Deputy McGee would package everything into a file and the case would stay open. They questioned everyone associated with the victims – friends and relatives, and those living in proximity to the murders. They looked for patterns; anything the victims had in common. They found *nothing!* After many frustrating weeks with nothing to show for their efforts but more murders, McGee took the day shift, and Rogers took the night patrol. But on an island the size of Manhattan, two people were nowhere near enough manpower. Citizen patrols were added and Rogers himself assigned the patrol routes – areas that had already proven popular with the killer, and other areas that were similar in terrain and isolation. No one ever saw anything.

Meanwhile, the people of Sanibel were frightened and distrustful. They jumped at stray noises and were startled by shadows. Doctor Wilson was seeing more PTSD and simple anxiety; depression was common also. At their weekly Monday meetings, the council members could discuss nothing else, so preoccupied was the island. Many islanders talked of leaving, and some actually did leave. Privation was one thing, but the random loss of life was quite another. A numbing resignation in the people was being born of a learned helplessness. Enthusiasm for sustainable transformation of the island community was waning.

It was against this backdrop that a total eclipse of the moon occurred on Sanibel. Most were not expecting the event, and to many it was an omen portending doom. Humans are generally capable of rationally assessing events that are not easily understood at first, but that is when their emotions will allow calm reasoning to occur. The eclipse brought forth primitive and superstitious thoughts and responses and frightened the bejeezus out of

102

everyone. Even those who knew what was happening as it happened were caught up in the gloom and hysteria.

March 29, 2025

The night offered no solace. It was pitch black because of the new moon. A solar eclipse earlier that day was not visible from south Florida, but the blackened moon did seem to affect the tides and the moods. Even Jesse and Beverly began locking their house.

Jesse was cleaning the dishes and pans while Beverly and Marti relaxed in the living room, sipping herbal tea. They had offered Marti some wine but she declined because Beverly could not have any. Jesse thought he saw movement in the garden, decided it was just the strange day holding sway, but went outside to check. He told the women, "I'm going out to get some air."

Beverly told him to be careful, but she also thought she was overreacting.

On the patio, Jesse listened to frogs and to leaves rustling in the breeze. He strained his eyes against the darkness, made worse by the house-glow. Somewhat satisfied he came back in and joined the women.

They talked until late. Marti was serving as Beverly's maid-of-honor, and although no date was set, everyone suspected it would be soon, almost any time. For one thing they were waiting for the mood to lighten, and people to not be so hard pressed with little things like the investigation of serial killings.

It was getting late and Marti rose to go home.

"Don't be silly, Marti," said Beverly. "We have lots of space."

"I know," said Marti. "I just would rather sleep in my own bed. Besides I live close. I will borrow a flashlight, though, if that's OK."

"Well at least let Jesse walk with you," offered.

Jesse hadn't said anything. He was conflicted. He couldn't be two places at once and if he had seen someone in the garden, he did not want

105

to leave Beverly. Still he didn't say anything. He was relieved when Marti refused the offer.

They stepped out into the dark night air. There was a light breeze off the Gulf, with the faint smell of salt and fish. Marti snapped on the flashlight and shown it around. The beam added reassurance.

"Where were you during the eclipse earlier," asked Marti. She was reminded of the dimming of the sun by the absence of any moonlight on this night.

"I was at the community kitchen doing clean-up," said Beverly. "Jesse was at Michael's office going over the forensic evidence." She regretted mentioning the danger that lurked out there as soon as she had said something. The one pattern that had emerged was how the killings seemed to all be at the same time in the late night, like about this time of day.

If Marti was bothered by the mention, she didn't let on. She said her goodbyes and gave out hugs. "I'll drop by tomorrow. You might want to go with me. Sharon wants me to cut her hair tomorrow and I think it needs it, don't you?"

"Indeed," agreed Beverly. And with that, Marti was off into the darkness for the four block walk home. Jesse and Beverly watched her disappear as the flashlight beam swung to and fro.

Unfortunately, they were not the only ones watching her leave. Jesse's suspicions were well founded. There *was* another someone hidden among the trees and towering shrubs, watching, waiting for an opportunity.

Jesse and Beverly could no longer see Marti. She had turned a corner. They stepped inside and bolted the door. The stalker had been watching them in particular, but Marti's departure and the deep darkness of the night had drawn him to follow her. It was she that he now stalked. *Even better*, he thought to himself. *Vengeance times three.*

Marti sensed that she was being watched. The wind in the trees, small mammals and rodents in the dense vegetation, tree frogs, even the distant surf – noises were everywhere, but none pointed to a stalker. Marti was uneasy, tense, and that grew to becoming worried. Halfway home a man approached, a muscular man with a purposeful stride, coming directly toward her on the same sidewalk. He was already close when Marti saw him in the darkened foreground. She slowed to a stop, trying to decide whether to turn and run back to Beverly and Jesse's.

As she started to make her move, he called out to her, "Marti, is that you? Are you OK? What are you doing out this time of night?"

"Jeffrey?" she called back. "Thank goodness it's you. What are you doing here?"

"I'm on patrol," he replied. "We are doing that every night now, you know, with the troubles and all. Let me walk you to your door."

"Much obliged," Marti accepted the offer gratefully. She hadn't seen much of Jeffrey since they were an item, before the dinner at the Mad Hatter, before that whole circle of friends dumped him like a hot potato after he giggled his admission of contributing to one of the world's greatest genocidal tragedies by selling munitions to African Muslims and making a bloody fortune in the process.

They walked along in silence, a continuation of the car ride home that fateful night. The mood was not lost on Jeffrey, but if he was upset anew, he did not show it. He seemed calm and pleasant to

Marti. Perhaps Jesse was right. Maybe Jeffrey was finding some maturity. He was certainly working hard as Sanibel's new sheriff.

When they arrived at Marti's door, they stood in an awkward silence. Should she invite him in? Should she rekindle the feelings they once felt for one another. *Too soon*, she thought.

Marti turned to face Jeffrey. "You are a life-saver. Thanks so much for seeing me home. With everything that has been going on, I have to admit I was worried and imagining all kinds of things out there in the dark."

"No problem. Do I need to stay a bit?" Jeffrey offered.

"No. I'll be fine now, thanks to you"

"Good night, then."

"Good night, Jeffrey. And thanks again."

She had unlocked the door, stepped in and was closing it when Jeffrey placed his foot in the gap, and pushed the door hard into Marti's forehead, knocking her down.

Marti was athletic, but she was no match for Jeffrey Roger's strength and training. Before he was in the NSA, he had gone through special forces training. Only his psychological profile suggesting sociopathic tendencies prevented him from serving among the elite. His reflexes and combat skills were first rate.

He placed his boot on her neck and pinned her down with ease and precision. He slowly lifted his foot, stood her up and told her that if she didn't cry out or try to struggle he would have no reason to hurt her. There was no one who would have heard her even if she screamed. The neighborhood was not well populated. They both knew that. He gently turned her around so that she faced away from him. He clamped his left hand over her mouth and his right arm across her breasts. She was surprised at the amount of strength he was showing as he pinned her to his chest. In his right hand was a military style knife. He did not need to reposition his forearm, only his wrist, to touch the tip of the blade to her neck. It was menacing, as intended, and Marti responded. Her nostrils flared and her pupils dilated. Her heart rate accelerated along with her respirations. She was going limp from helplessness when Jeffrey whispered hotly in her ear.

"First," he said, "I do *not* forgive you for betraying me that night. I do not forgive any of you, and neither do the gods. Why do you think Sanibel crumbled?"

"Second, the sheriff – that's me – is also the serial killer that he is in charge of investigating." Jeffrey's voice dripped with irony.

"And *third!*" he tightened his grip dramatically with the utterance in order to emphasize the futility of any effort to struggle. "You are about to die."

Not only could Marti not struggle, she couldn't breathe, so tight was Jeffrey's grip across her chest. When he released it for a second, she still could not breathe because of the left hand covering her mouth and nose. Then came the upward thrust of the knife into the heart, penetrating the ventricle from below the sternum. The blood from the ventricle flowed into the pericardial sac, creating a cardiac tapenade that squeezed the heart and kept it from pumping blood to the brain. That alone would have killed her if the ventricular arrhythmia hadn't.

He held her like that, knife inserted to the hilt, her feet inches above the ground, feeling the life leave her body, and leaving it flaccid. Jeffrey lowered his ex-lover to the floor gently, and stabbed her several more times, not in anger, but methodically. She must look exactly like the others, he reasoned. She was not exactly like the others, he knew. The first ones had been strangers and she was personal, but it must appear that she was part of a random pattern, not a steppingstone to Beverly and Jesse. *They* had to die, too, but all in good time. Motive was strong; still waiting for opportunity.

Meanwhile, he must prepare for the investigation. *Who will find her? Jesse or Beverly or both when she doesn't show tomorrow, and they check on her. What will they find? A home invasion indistinguishable from the other two.*

Jeffrey let himself out the back door, broke the small window pane nearest the door knob with the butt of his knife handle so that the glass landed inside the house, and used the back of the blade to remove the jagged shards of glass from the door. He then took inventory. No fingerprints; no DNA. He would leave the door unlocked. The "killer" would have had no reason to lock it back after he left. He could think of no reason to go back inside.

Sheriff Rogers resumed his night patrol. The entire murder took surprisingly little time.

March 31, 2025

Beverly was the second one to get up and out of bed again. The change in routines was part amusing and part annoying. She found Jesse on the patio with a surprise guest, Dr. Michael Wilson. He had moved into Alison's house soon after the invasion. His place was destroyed, like so many others, by indiscriminate shelling.

Michael and Alison had been roommates since their engagement. Their home was not reflective of their combined means, but it was tasteful, comfortable, big enough, and on the Gulf. It was very well appointed with mementos of Ali's travels and Michael's eye for art, although his more valuable pieces did not survive the onslaught.

The gentlemen stood when Beverly approached, and Jesse gave her a big hug. Beverly greeted Michael warmly, asked about Alison, asked if the wedding date was set, and asked, "So what else is happening?" Local news had its own network. This morning they had a reliable source.

Michael assured them that other than the electrical power being off since yesterday morning that things were generally good. Fishing was a thriving enterprise and a barter economy had developed and thrived – services and goods of a rich variety. There were no new murders to report.

Jesse spoke the obvious in order to direct the conversation. "The mainlanders are again cutting power, despite payment, despite a lot of payment."

"That answers one question I had," said Michael. "…the part about as to why. It would seem that it is not about the money. It is more of a question of retribution. They want a bigger piece of flesh."

"I must confess," said Jesse. "I have been trying to avoid going to Fort Myers. I don't know or trust people there and I am usually a pretty 'glass half-full' kind of person. I think it is time, though – or past time – for us to try diplomacy."

"I agree," said Michael.

114

"I don't," said Beverly. She was worried about his safe return and felt vulnerable just thinking about it.

"Maybe if you get Jeffrey to go with you," Michael offered as a suggestion to Jesse.

"Yes," agreed Beverly. "Safety in numbers."

She was careful not to suggest that her Ph.D. husband-to-be was not the most combat-ready specimen on the island, but she knew his strengths lay elsewhere.

After another round or two of problem solving – there was nothing to be done about crop irrigation until the electricity for the pumping station could be made more secure – Michael rose to go "check on his office".

Jesse followed suit. "Jeffrey should be at home. He is on night patrol schedule. I will have to wake him. I hope he has gotten some sleep."

The three were clearing dishes from the patio table when Sharon Welker rounded the corner of the house and was greeted warmly.

"Look who is out and about," smiled Beverly.

"Has anyone seen Marti?" Sharon asked. "She was supposed to cut my hair yesterday and we never hooked up."

"Did you check her house?" asked Beverly.

"No, I have been out of touch and I don't know where she lives now after all of the rearrangement and people moving here and there."

"I will take you there," offered Beverly. "This party is breaking up anyway. Just let me get some clothes on."

"Stop by and get Alison," suggested Michael. "She isn't on landscaping duty today, and was talking about Sharon the other day, and all the time they used to spend together. She would enjoy getting out."

"Will do," Beverly agreed, and went inside to change clothes.

.   .   .   .   .

Michael and Jesse left together on bicycles, but went separate directions soon after they came to Periwinkle Drive. Jesse arrived at Jeffrey Roger's condominium and rang the bell. There was no

116

response and Jesse remembered that there might not be any electricity. He knocked with the brass knocker centered on the large red 6-paneled door. He waited, listened in silence, and knocked again; he waited, listened, and knocked insistently. He heard a muffled noise.

"Coming," said Jeffrey.

The door opened slowly revealing a sleepy sheriff in uncharacteristic casual attire.

"Where are the bunny slippers?" Jesse teased.

"They hopped away," Jeffrey played along. "What's up?" Jeffrey was sure they had found Marti. It wouldn't take long. *No,* he thought. *Jesse is too calm and collected. It's not about that.*

"I know you can't have gotten much sleep, but do you feel up to going with me to Fort Myers? I need to negotiate with somebody there about the electricity."

"Sure Jesse. Anything. Let me get dressed. It turns out the sheriff's department has a boat."

"Perfect," replied Jesse appreciatively.

"Come in and make yourself comfortable. We can run by the station and get the keys, and then head for the marina."

117

Minutes later they were biking to the station. Russell was there and fixed them some sandwiches and coffee. There was nothing to report, he told Jeffrey.

The boat was a sturdy craft with spotlights and a large motor. It made the crossing through Pine Island Sound in a short period of time, but long enough for them to finish their lunch and coffee, and long enough to chat about Jesse's upcoming marriage. Jeffrey seemed particularly happy for the couple.

They maneuvered the craft, throttled back to avoid a wake, into a marina near Fort Myers. Neither was at all familiar with the location or the people. They would have preferred to stay incognito themselves, but the boat was labeled with *Sheriff's Department, Sanibel Island,* so it was not like they could conceal their identities. Jeffrey was in uniform, so there was a clue as well.

A man with military bearing presented himself. "Sheriff, how can we help you?" he said, addressing the man in uniform and ignoring Jesse.

"I guess we would like to see the man in charge," replied Jeffrey.

"The 'man in charge' is a woman," the man answered wryly, but I can take you to her.

The three were joined by three others. Jesse and Jeffrey were separated into matching vehicles, each accompanied by two guards. The black Toyota FJ Cruisers were luxurious and powerful vehicles, but this convoy did not have the feel of anything remotely welcoming. Jeffrey and Jesse were being taken prisoner and it *did* feel like *that*.

They arrived at a former condominium complex that had been converted to military quarters. Jesse was taken in one direction, Jeffrey in another. *So much for safety in numbers,* thought Jesse.

Jesse was taken to a stereotypical interview room with two metal chairs facing each other, separated by a metal table. There was no mirrored wall for surveillance and no camera that Jesse could see. *What happens in Fort Myers, stays in Fort Myers.* Jesse feared that he would not keep his sense of humor much longer. He decided to meditate.

.　　.　　.　　.　　.

Beverly and Sharon knocked a number of times on Alison's door. She was in the studio working on a project and couldn't hear them at first.

"Come in. Come in," Alison squealed with delight.

"Hey, girl," said Sharon, obviously delighted to see her old friend. "How about a round of *mango tangos*."

"Definitely that can be arranged," said Alison, gleefully remembering happier days. "What brings you two here?"

"We were headed over to Marti's, and thought maybe you would like to join us," said Beverly.

"Yes, of course," replied Alison. "But I can be decadent, too. I don't think I have any mango juice but would you like some pineapple juice and rum?"

"Why not?" replied Sharon. "Sure."

"None for me," said Beverly. "I gave up pineapple juice for Lent."

"Lent began March 5, young lady," replied Alison. "Your 40 days of fasting and payments are going to crimp your style for several weeks yet."

"Alright then," Beverly went along. "I shall have your pineapple juice. But do hold the rum."

120

"You got it, sweetie," said Alison, looking at Beverly suspiciously, suspecting to see a larger baby bump where there was almost none."

"How far along are you?" Sharon asked without hesitation or doubt.

"Three months, I think, maybe four. I keep thinking I will go see Michael and get a more accurate reading on that."

"Oh, honey, congratulations," said Alison.

The friends enjoyed a group hug and sat for a while in Alison's shaded porch with screens on three sides.

"Sorry the ceiling fan is not working. Seems that we cannot rely on electricity from the mainland. Did Michael stop by your place, Beverly? I know he was worried yesterday when he was doing minor surgery on a patient and the electricity failed. He had to move the procedure into the sunlight. It did okay, but he was worried about the next time."

"Yes," replied Beverly. "I think the plan is for Jesse and Jeffrey to go to Fort Myers and see if they can negotiate with them. Jesse is worried that they want revenge more than they want any kind of money."

"If that's the case," Alison said after some thought, "then I am afraid of what they might run up against."

"Exactly," said Beverly, pleased that someone else shared her concerns.

Sharon said nothing, but she struggled to suppress the emotions that stayed just below the surface ever since her ordeal as a result of the invasion. The happiness generated by the reunion grew more tenuous, as concerns turned to worry.

"Come my broody hens. Let's go for a walk," suggested Alison. "Finish your drinks."

.   .   .   .   .

Jeffrey was the first to encounter Major Maxwell. The interrogation room was an ample 10' x 12' space. The walls were gray; the chairs and tables were dark gray. Maj. Maxwell's uniform was black. Jeffrey Roger's uniform was tan. It was the only color in the room.

"What are you boys doing here?" asked the major. "You must know that you are not welcome."

"We just came to talk," replied Rogers. "We don't want any trouble."

"We're not interested in anything you have to say. And you have found trouble whether you wanted it or not."

"Let's get it over with," said Rogers impatiently. "The other guy's the diplomat. I am just the stooge."

"Well, stand up, stooge," said Maj. Maxwell. Jeffrey obliged, and a small squadron of burly volunteers crowded the room.

As Jeffrey was standing, he was flanked by two large men who secured his arms near the shoulders and held him close.

"Can I fight back, or will that get me killed?" asked Jeffrey, with a swagger that few people could have genuinely expressed.

"Ordinarily I would tell you 'fight back and you will die', but I suspect you know that's the likely outcome anyway. What the hell," Maj. Maxwell sneered at Jeffrey. "Let's see what you got." He turned to the men in the room. "Who wants first dibs?"

One of the men closest to Rogers took a step forward and delivered a kick, heel first, to the mid abdomen. Jeffrey saw it coming and tightened his muscles, taking the blow in stride. He pushed off with 1 foot, giving his entire weight to the startled men holding his shoulders, and exploded the man's face with a deft kick of his own. As the two that had been holding him struggled to regain their balance, Jeffrey slipped their grips, turned and palmed their faces gripping their heads like they were melons and smashed their heads, once, twice, into the wall. They would not be getting back up. The three left standing braced themselves, but too late. Jeffrey rushed them, and in a series of spins, kicks, and knuckle blows to vital neck and facial features, he left their bodies still or moving slowly in pain on the floor of the interrogation room.

Jeffrey Rogers picked up one of the metal chairs and sat back down the metal table across from Maj. Maxwell. "I've got nothing much to say," he said.

"You are not a small time sheriff, are you?" said Maxwell rhetorically.

"Former covert operative," Rogers replied.

Maxwell rose, and locked the door behind him as he left. The bodies were still on the floor. Rogers did not check on any of them. He thought they all would make it. He had not tried to kill any of them, although he could have. He thought it would not have been wise under the circumstance. Still he did not make any new friends that afternoon.

.　　　.　　　.　　　.　　　.

Alison and Sharon had been chatting sometimes giggly on the way to Marti's. Beverly was the quiet one, still worried about Jesse.

When they got to Marti's house, it was Beverly who knocked. There was no answer and she knocked again. She did not try the door. That would have been presumptive. Rather the three women walked around back to see if Marti might be on the patio. It could explain why she did not answer the door. What they found instead was a door with a broken pane of glass. Instantly they were gripped fear and concern. They hurried to the door and tried it. It was not locked. Beverly pulled it open and said to the others, "Be careful of the broken glass."

"Marti!" They all called out.

Stepping into the living room, they could immediately see her on the floor of the foyer, partly in the kitchenette, lying twisted in a pool of her own blood. They were horrified! They stepped back, wailing and holding each other in grief. They all three were hyperventilating. Terrified they went outside the way they had come in. "Don't touch anything," cautioned Beverly.

"Alison take Sharon back to your place," instructed Beverly. "I'll take the bicycle and find Sheriff Rogers or his deputy." Beverly was the youngest, but the least hysterical. The others agreed and she was off.

As she rode, she could see only blurry images of the sidewalks and people. Tears filled her eyes and her sobbing shook her body and the bicycle. In spite of that she paddled hard and fast. She arrived at the station and found Deputy Magee doing paperwork.

"Beverly, oh I mean, Mrs. O'Connell," said Russell. "What is the matter? How can I help you?"

Beverly could hardly respond. She was only moderately winded from the bicycle ride, but the hysteria over finding her best friend dead was flooding her like a tidal wave. She was sobbing and shaking, and poor Russell had no clue how to console her. "She's dead," Beverly finally blurted

126

out the essential message. "Marti Leinhart is dead. There has been another murder. It's horrible. She's in her own home lying in her own blood. What is wrong with this horrible, horrible world?"

"I'll go there now," Russell said. It was the only reassurance he could offer. "Do you want to come with me? I don't think you should be alone. You can show me what you found when you got there if you feel up to it."

"I can go with you, but I cannot go in. Not again."

"There's no reason you should have to go back in," assured Russell. "When did you see her last?"

"Two nights ago," said Beverly. "She was helping me plan my wedding, and we were laughing about everything. She was my best friend. It is just not right. It's not fair." Beverly began to cry. "Where's Jesse. I want Jesse." She was really losing control now.

"Jesse and Sheriff Rogers took the boat over to Fort Myers," said Deputy Magee. "They went to negotiate about the island's electricity. I don't know when they will get back. I don't think *they* knew."

Beverly began to wail. Russell stepped over to her and placed his arms around her uncertainly. He thought it was the right thing to do but never knew delicate things like boundaries. Beverly was beyond caring. She was inconsolable. Nothing could be worse than this. Everything on this island had become so difficult. People were pulling together for survival, but crisis after crisis made life feel like one step forward and two steps back. Her best friend was dead. She was engaged to the best man she had ever met, and she loved him dearly, but what if he was to be killed while he was at Fort Myers? She was pregnant and overjoyed about that, but what if something happened to the baby? Her life was falling apart, and she desperately needed things back to normal.

.   .   .   .   .

Jesse was sitting on the table in full lotus position when Major Maxwell entered. He opened his eyes abruptly but nothing else moved.

"You two are polar opposites," Maxwell observed with wry amusement.

Jesse swung around lightly and stood beside the table. "Good afternoon, Major," he said, judging by the uniform.

"And who are you?" challenged the major.

"Jesse O'Connell, Major."

"Who are you to me?"

"I am the man who pays Fort Myers for the electricity provided to Sanibel."

"You have gold, then?" Maxwell inquired.

"I have some. It's in the Caymans."

"Smart. What is your office on Sanibel?"

"Pardon?"

"Mayor? City Executive, or what?"

"Oh, okay. Uh... Volunteer?"

"You're a volunteer."

"That's right."

"Did you volunteer to die?"

"I hope not."

"What is your background?"

"I have a Ph.D. in philosophy. Is that what you are asking?"

"Any special forces background? Or Military?"

"Lord, no. No weapons skills at all. I can sail a boat, ride a bike..."

"Are you messing with me"

"No, Major. I'm just trying to answer the questions as I understand them."

Major Maxwell rapped his knuckles on the door once and six large men entered, "These are *our* volunteers, Dr. O'Connell. They all lost loved ones when your security forces massacred their settlement."

"That was terrible. I mourned their losses and prayed for them in my way, but I had no knowledge it was going to happen and no control over those decisions. I am sorry."

"Not as sorry as you are about to be."

"Wait. You would be exacting your revenge on someone who had nothing to do with that. What is the point?"

"You profess innocence. That's easy enough to do, and who wouldn't to save himself a beating that he may or may not survive? But think again. You paid top dollar to live on Sanibel under the protection of your mercenaries. Those mercs were ruthless if they captured one of us, and your ilk paid for that."

"That's true, but I lived on Sanibel long before it was flooded by… you know, the über-rich."

"Still," persisted Maxwell. "You stayed and you paid. You had *privilege*."

Jesse was slow to respond. "That's true. I was complicit... guilty by association."

"Gentlemen?" said Maxwell, granting them access to the islander.

The closest man stepped forward and buried his fist into Jesse's abdomen, doubling him over and knocking the wind out of him.

"This is so not necessary," pleaded Jesse.

"You may fight back, if you wish," offered Maxwell.

"Thank you, no. I'm afraid that isn't my..."

The first man threw a second punch, this time to the side of Jesse's face. It spun him to the ground, and he did not get up. The other five men were disappointed that they didn't get their chance. One at a time they kicked at his unconscious body, sometimes breaking a rib, sometimes only a frustrated gesture. They knew he wasn't the enemy.

Jesse stirred slowly and painfully as he regained consciousness. The air was dank and the room was pitch dark. There was no sound other than his heartbeat. *Still alive,* he thought. He moved; he winced with pain. He moved another way; he

131

winced with pain in another location. He took a breath; he gasped with the pain of a rib broken in his left chest. He decided to lie still and get a little more sleep.

Jesse was jolted awake by the sound of the iron door opening. Major Maxwell and his men had come to retrieve him. They roughly lifted Jesse to a standing position, ignoring his expressions of pain and protest.

"Don't you want to know where we are taking you?" asked Maxwell.

"I'll find out when we get there," said Jesse. He suspected another beating. It was all he could feel right now. Was there any place on him that did not hurt? It was difficult to think about anything else.

They passed along several corridors and through two doors that required remote assistance to open. At the third door requiring someone to buzz them in, Jesse decided they had gone overboard on security. He also felt they were taking him to the seventh level of hell, never to return.

Jesse could hardly walk. He tried not to show his pain, but he recognized that he had been beaten a lot more than he remembered. He suddenly felt very light-headed and weak. He was going to be sick, he realized, as he bent over and purged his stomach of its contents. He fell to one knee and had a close look at the pool of blood and vomit he had just created. He was jerked by his painful arm back to standing.

"Die, if you need to," said the unsympathetic major. "Save us some trouble later."

They arrived at a door, knocked and entered on command.

"This is our *volunteer*, Colonel." Major Maxwell shoved Jesse a step toward Colonel Beasley's desk and left. Two of his men stayed behind.

"What brings you behind enemy lines, O'Connell?" asked Col. Beasley.

"I came to negotiate about our electricity," Jesse spoke in swallow gasps and a hoarse whisper. He was surprised how the exertion to walk here had exhausted him. "May I sit down?" he asked.

"Sure. Sit!" said the colonel. "What is your offer?"

"Sanibel is trying to become self-sufficient. We need water for crops. For that we need electricity for our desalinization plant. We need reliable electricity. I came to ask you, or someone, what you need in return. Also, we are not your enemy. Your enemies are dead. We are a pathetic defeated lot, just trying to hold our heads up and just get by with what little we were left."

"You have gold, I am told."

"Yes. Gold bullion at a bank in the Cayman Islands. But we cannot eat gold."

"How much gold?" asked Beasley.

"Some. I'm not sure," replied Jesse, not wanting to reveal his hand this early in the poker game. "It has been what has backed the electronic transfers you have been getting from us."

"What are you offering, exactly?"

"I am just trying to find out what it will take to keep the power on," said Jesse wearily, just before he passed out again.

.   .   .   .   .

Russell and Beverly parked their bikes in Marti's yard. "Just wait here," he suggested. "I'll be back after I've had a chance to look around. I'll probably have some questions for you then. Also, don't let anyone else in. It is a secure crime scene now."

Beverly nodded, subdued. She wanted no part of this or any other "crime scene".

Russell tried the front door. It was open. "Did she ever lock her doors?" he turned to ask Beverly.

"Never," she replied. "She loved and trusted everyone. She was such a good person. That's what makes this all the more tragic."

Russell went in but did not close the door. He needed the light. He was wearing gloves but did not touch the corpse. That job was left for Dr. Wilson. When he got to the back door, he noticed the broken glass on the floor and the missing pane in the door. *Why would anyone need to break the glass if the door was unlocked?* He wondered. *Why take the risk of alerting someone to the invasion. The killer had been so careful in the past – attention to detail, no physical clues – why would he not do something so basic as to check a door to see if it were locked?*

Though the body was not touched, it raised questions, too. *She was dressed nicely, with jewelry even. She was going out or had just been out with friends. Why the foyer? It would appear she had just let somebody in her house, but again, why the broken glass at the back door? Something didn't add up.* Russell would be glad when Jeffrey got back to help him with these questions.

Russell returned to where Beverly was sitting in a lawn chair. She was exhausted emotionally and physically. She did not want to answer any questions, but she knew she had to.

Did you say Marti was at your house night before last?" asked Russell.

"That's right.

"Was she wearing what she has on now?"

"Yes."

"That narrows the time of death," Russell speculated. He didn't have any more questions at the present, he told Beverly, and she was glad. She retrieved her bike and pedaled homeward. *Jesse*, she thought to herself. *Come home to me. I need you.*

.   .   .   .   .

When Jesse awoke this time, he was in a much brighter and cleaner place. His bed had sheets and a cover. He still had pain all over, but some things never seem to change. He also had intravenous fluids infusing into a vein in his left arm. He also had several electronic chest leads connecting, perhaps by Bluetooth, to monitors that beeped and chimed whimsically. He was in a hospital ward.

He felt terrible, weak, and confused, and in pain – always in pain. He tried to turn and held to a bed rail to support his effort. The painful areas now felt as if they were ripping, and he fell back supine as if he had over exerted. His breathing did become more labored, and his broken ribs tortured him from the effort. His mouth was dry.

A nurse appeared at his bedside. He told Jesse to try to lie still. He told Jesse that he had had surgery to remove his spleen, and that he was very anemic. He told Jesse that he would like to give him something for pain, but that it was not permitted.

Jesse understood much of what he was told. He was awake but not fully aware of his circumstances. He fell back asleep, but it was a fitful sleep.

April 1, 2025

Jesse was awakened, this time, by a small surgical team of doctors. They removed bandages from his left upper abdomen, inspected and smelled the area, and palpated gently with experienced fingertips. They reviewed vital signs, asked the nurse about urine output, and inquired as to various potential post op problems. It was only then that they noticed that their patient was awake and looking at them.

"How are you feeling?" asked the taller, older surgeon.

"I feel like hell," replied Jesse.

The team ignored him after that. They left for the nurse's station to compile Jesse's daily statistics in the format of a progress note. Most of the information was populated electronically. All that was left for them was to check its accuracy and signoff on the attestation.

Jesse called out from his bed, "can anyone tell me where I am and what has happened to me?"

A young doctor returned to his bedside. "You are in Lee County Memorial Hospital," he said. "You were beaten and kicked by a group of men who lost loved ones in the senseless slaughter of civilians that your people on Sanibel carried out a little over a year ago. One or more of those kicks caused your spleen to rupture. Consider it payback for your hubris. The good news for you is that the militia sent you to the hospital rather than let you bleed to death at their headquarters. Why they didn't just kill you, I don't understand. I lost people that day, too."

Before he left Jesse, the young doctor put his hand precisely over Jesse's two broken ribs and gave them a sharp push inward, causing Jesse to recoil and wince. "Have a nice day," he said bitterly.

As the days went by, and Jesse found it easier to eat and to sit for short periods in a bedside chair. A man from physical therapy helped him regain the strength to walk. It seemed that everyone assigned to him had lost a friend or relative in the massacre along the Caloosahatchee River. Jesse was routinely treated roughly.

After a week he was given a pneumonia vaccination and a Covid-19/21 booster and was transferred to a holding cell at militia headquarters in Fort Myers. He received food and bandages, and scant attention. After a few more weeks he was able to do light calisthenics, like push-ups against his cell wall. Deep knee bends and rotational twisting of the torso came soon afterwards.

April 27, 2025

Jesse was feeling stronger when two men came and escorted him to Col. Beasley's office.

"Remember me?" asked the colonel.

"You're Col. Beasley," replied Jesse.

"That's right. Sit in the chair and remain quiet. I am taking you to see the director in a bit."

Jesse did as he was told, but after maintaining his silence for 15 or 20 minutes he let his mind wander. Forgetting decorum, he asked a question that had been on his mind. "Where is Jeffrey Rogers?"

141

"He's safe," replied Beasley without looking up from his papers. No more was said.

After another period of silence, the door opened and a man said to Beasley, "The director can see him now."

Beasley stood up and Jesse followed suit. The three men walked some distance to another wing in the complex where richly paneled wooden doors opened to reveal a spacious and well-appointed office, clearly that of an executive. Jesse was brought to the chairs facing the man's desk, and with a strong hand on his shoulder he was encouraged to sit.

"I hear you have been unwell," began the director. "I hear also that you had little personally to do with the massacre at the Caloosahatchee River. I understand also that you came here to talk about securing reliable electricity for Sanibel. Do I hear correctly?"

"That pretty well sums it up," said Jesse. He was never one to use more words than were necessary, so he appreciated the director's brevity.

The director was brief by virtue of administrative efficiency. He was an accomplished beaurocrat. "What are you paying now for the limited kilowatt-hours that we are sending your way?"

"$25,000 a month in gold-secured electronic bank credits," Jesse replied.

"And how much more power is it that you think you will need to keep the lights on and the water flowing without interruption?"

"Perhaps twice as much as we are getting now."

"That's less than I thought you would ask for," said the director. "I think we can reach a deal."

"What do you want from us?" asked Jesse.

"$100,000 in gold bullion and $60,000 a month in electronic bank credits," replied the director.

"I will have to travel to the Grand Cayman's to get the physical gold," said Jesse. "I will need some time to heal before I can actually go get the gold. The electronic bank credits I can authorize by satellite phone as soon as I get back to Sanibel. Are these terms acceptable?"

"Yes," agreed the director. "We have continued to provide electricity while you are recuperating. We can double the amount provided when we receive the increase in bank credits. I know you are in no condition to sail now because of your injuries, so we will give you until August 1, slightly more than three months, to provide the gold bullion, but the new amount with interest because of the delay is $120,000. Agreed?"

"Agreed," said Jesse, and he offered his hand, outstretched, to seal the deal.

The director looked at his hand, then his face, then back to the work on his desk. Jesse was dismissed without another word.

"When can I leave for Sanibel?" Jesse asked Beasley as they walked down the walkway away from the director's office.

"We can take you tomorrow afternoon. Your friend went back last night in the boat you came over on. He seemed to be in too much of a hurry to wait for you. He probably thought we would take another of his teeth, but there wasn't any point. He really didn't know anything that we didn't already know."

.   .   .   .   .

Beverly was especially lonely. She did get word that Jeffrey returned alone in the police boat that he and Jesse had taken to Fort Myers. She did not know if this meant that Jesse would soon be released also. She had heard that Jeffrey expected that he would, and soon, but Beverly could not depend on rumors. Still she has reason for hope, and hope right now represented everything to her. Jesse was her life, her one love, the father of their child, and the man of her dreams.

During the weeks when she did not know if he was dead or alive, Beverly eulogized and idealized Jesse. In her mind Jesse had become the perfect man: strong, handsome, a virile lover, gentle, a good listener, tender and careful with respect to the feelings of others, intelligent, respectful, wise, and always, he always strove to do what was right. Jesse was not just a good man, he was the best man she could imagine. She ached for Jesse deep in her soul. She agonized for his safe return. Tonight especially, with hope in ascendancy, she needed her man.

Beverly dined alone, actively avoiding her usual glass of wine that had become an evening routine prior to her pregnancy. She treated herself to peanut butter. Once a week she baked bread. It was not difficult. She and her grandmother used to bake bread together. The house always smelled so good afterwards. Tonight, she treated herself to peanut butter on fresh baked bread with a large spoonful of grape jelly. She wished she had some 2% milk for herself but also for the baby. Beverly thought that she could see a "baby bump" a month ago, but she thought it must be clearly obvious to even the most casual observer now. She suspected that she might be five months along. With that thought she found her prenatal vitamins and took one.

While standing at the kitchen window by her sink, Beverly thought she caught a glimpse of movement. Primal fear and thoughts of Marti swept over her. She wished she had a gun, but the Army of the Association took all weapons. As far as she knew, there were none left on Sanibel. She thought she remembered one on Jesse's sailboat.

Beverly turned on the patio lights, saw nothing, and turned them off again. To view the garden grounds beyond the patio, she could see better with the lights off anyway, usually, but tonight the new moon offered precious little illumination. She turned out the lights in her kitchen and strained for another glimpse of anything, any motion, no matter how subtle. But it was *dark* and there was nothing. It was neither more fearsome nor was it more reassuring. Jesse's sailboat, *Serenity,* was anchored in a nearby canal in the other direction, out the front door across the street and across one small yard. Beverly was an adequate marksman. The more she thought about the gun, the more she was certain that she needed it.

Jeffrey was settled comfortably in a pine thicket toward the back of Jesse and Beverly's 3 ½ acre property. The torture he had endured at the hands of the militia in Fort Myers was mild compared to the throbbing need to kill again. He had not had to wait more than a month since his first foray into the killing spree. Like an addict, the compulsion to kill was a force that could not be denied. It must be obeyed. It was a master without parallel or equal. Jeffrey was its slave.

Beverly had spent time staring out windows in all directions. She decided it was safe to go check *Serenity* for the Glock that Jesse kept on the boat. He could have moved it and not told her. He could've thrown it away in a pithy revulsion of all things violent. All Beverly knew was that she would feel

147

safer having the gun, at least until Jesse was back home.

Beverly opened the front door slowly. There were no lights on in the house to draw attention. She closed it just as slowly and quietly before she started down the drive toward the street.

Where is she going this time of night? wondered Jeffrey. *This is my lucky night.* His pupils dilated with excitement as he moved toward her in stealth mode.

As Beverly approached the trees behind which he maintained his cover, Jeffrey tried to decide whether to jump out in front of her or swing around behind her, securing her mouth and nose with his left hand and pinning her to him with his right, as he had done with so many others. *Yes*, he thought, *stay with what has worked.* There was no more time for planning. Beverly was upon him now, two steps from the tree, now one. *Now!*

Jeffrey made his move. He catapulted himself around the tree behind her and reached for her mouth with his left hand. As he did Beverly sensed his actions, she heard a brush with the tree and felt the wind of his motion. When Jeffrey made his move, Beverly made hers. She lurched forward and began to run. Jeffrey's hand did little more than

148

brush her left neck with his fingertips. She abandoned the thought of *Serenity* and the gun, turned right onto the road and hit full stride. She was fast and she had skills honed in college and maintained over the years. Jeffrey was fast also, but weeks of being caged and tortured had deconditioned him just enough for him to lose his edge. Beverly lengthened the distance between them by a full stride, then two strides.

Jeffrey had a dilemma. He was confident he could catch her despite her quick start advantage. But he also had doubts. What if she got away, and even worse, what if she glanced back at him long enough to recognize him? Jeffrey could never allow himself to be recognized.

Beverly ran fast and hard as Jeffrey pulled back and disappeared into the shrubbery. Beverly was not taking any chances. She ran until she came to Alison and Michael's house where she pounded on the door. They responded to the urgent pounding, and Alison took the sobbing Beverly by the shoulders and led her to the living room sofa, while Michael shined a flashlight in all directions from the doorstep. Satisfied, he stepped back inside and locked the door.

Beverly sobbed, and with a quiver in her voice, she told them about the attack, the trauma of finding Marti, the aching for Jesse, and the fear that something will happen to her, and therefore her baby.

Michael handed her a glass of water and said, "I hadn't realized you were pregnant until just now. Nobody tells me anything."

Alison looked at him sympathetically and pouted about how pitiful he was. *Poor little baby*. But her conversation and attention stayed with Beverly. After an hour of comforting tea and sympathy, both Michael and Alison insisted that Beverly spend the night there with them. Beverly did not argue. She had been down that road before, but on the side of the hostess, and she knew how that turned out when the offer was declined.

April 28, 2025

The next morning over breakfast, Beverly swore the two to secrecy regarding the attack. She had not seen anything that would assist in the investigation, and she did not want Jesse worrying about her and the baby any more than he already did.

Michael agreed to tell no one about the attack, but he insisted that Beverly come by his office for a prenatal exam. She said she would be there this afternoon. She had been intending to set up an appointment, but one thing seem to lead to two others, and she had not managed to follow through. Today would be as good a time as any.

.   .   .   .   .

For Jesse, today was the day. After a month of captivity that included being beaten, nearly to death, Jesse was being escorted to a boat that would take him to Sanibel Island. His companion was a congenial sort of person, certainly more pleasant than almost anyone else he had met at Fort Myers. It had seemed to Jesse that people were calling in political favors for the privilege of being allowed to "take care of" the Islander.

They arrived at the Marina where several of Fort Myers' militia were waiting to say goodbye. Jesse feared that he was in for one more beating. He was pleasantly surprised when they nodded to him as a measure of respect and wished him well. Apparently, word had spread that Jesse was the nicer one of the two, and a standup guy.

As the boat slapped across the bay at high speed, Jesse turned to his companion and asked, "You're not going to drown me out here, are you?"

The man laughed a gentle laugh and replied, "No, Mr. O'Connell. I think it is fair to say that you have won us over with your honesty. You have the way about you, as they say. For all of the retribution we showed you at the beginning, there are those among us who believe, now that Island Security is gone, we can begin working with Sanibel again. We could start slow – a little trading, maybe a weekly mail boat or ferry service the way it used to be. Who knows? This could be the start of something."

They arrived at a marina on Sanibel. Barefoot Chuck came to meet them and help tie the boat to moorings. The conversations were short because Jesse was in a hurry to find Beverly.

"There are bikes in the usual place," called Barefoot Chuck as Jesse made his way uphill to the parking area.

Jesse pedaled as fast as his aching torso and limbs would carry him. He arrived at the house, but a quick search revealed that Beverly was out and about. He went to the community kitchen where she sometimes volunteered. Someone told him to check at Dr. Wilson's.

"Is she hurt," asked Jesse with obvious concern.

"Not as far as I know" was the response. "Something else maybe."

At Dr. Wilson's, Jesse leaned his bike against the stairs to the front porch and hurried through the door. "Michael," he called. "Beverly. Is anybody here?"

"Jesseee!" cried Beverly, too excited to stay on the ultrasound exam table.

"We're back here, Jesse," Michael called out. "Better get back here before…"

"Before what?" asked Jesse as he burst into the exam room.

"Before I can finish the sentence apparently," said Michael Wilson. "Now you two behave long enough for me to finish taking these baby pictures."

"Oh my God," said Jesse. "Something like this really makes it real, doesn't it?"

"Indeed it does, my love. It does indeed," agreed Beverly. And they stared into each other's eyes, melting and consummated, silent as Dr. Wilson finished the ultrasound of the baby.

"Everything looks all right," said Wilson cleaning the jelly from Beverly's abdomen.

"Everything *is* all right, now," said Jesse.

"Amen to that!" agreed Beverly.

"I would not want to be on the roller coaster ride you two are taking for anything," said Dr. Wilson. "Beverly you can get dressed. Jesse you can step into the next room and let me have a look at you. Jeffrey already told me you were minus a spleen."

"Minus a what?" exclaimed Beverly. "Jesse, what happened?"

"There will be time for that," said Wilson to Beverly, "and time for news that *we* have and *Jesse* doesn't, but first you get dressed, and you, Jesse, come with me."

In the exam room, Jesse took his shirt off and sat on the exam table, but Dr. Wilson wanted to check him head to toe. "Pants, too," said Wilson.

"Head is alright; a few healing contusions. No teeth missing. Jeffrey had had five teeth extracted, at different times and with wildly varying skill levels," Michael shared with Jesse. *HIPAA be damned.* "He had some fingernails pulled off too. All right, back to you. Neck is normal, trachea midline. Let's listen to your lungs… They are clear. Heart… Good. Abdomen… Soft, nontender. Left upper quadrant has this curvilinear surgical scar. It is healing well. No pus, no heat or erythema, no odor. Liver… small, not palpable. Extremities seem intact. Full range of motion. Clavicles are intact, nontender. Ribs, ouch, sorry, two maybe three ribs fractured in the left anterior axillary line."

After the exam, Jesse and Beverly met with Dr. Wilson in his consultation room. It was paneled

155

with rich colored woods, mostly cherry, and contained the books of a bygone era.

Jesse began, "Beverly told me about Marti. I just can't believe it."

"None of us can," replied Michael. "Did Beverly tell you that it was she who found Marti? She also needs to open up about how hard it has been on her not knowing if you were dead or alive."

"Everything's fine now," said Beverly, wanting it to be true.

"The hell it is," said Michael. "I am sure both of you are going to be as good as new, but you both have some things to work through. I know somebody you can talk to, alone or together. I am going to give you her name, but I want you to take the time to heal, and I want you to talk to someone. If it's not Melissa, it can be someone else, but talk to *someone*."

"I appreciate your concern, Michael," said Jesse, "and we will. But right now the only person I'm interested in talking to is sitting right here. If anybody needs me, I'm not back yet. I'll see you and the others at the Monday Council meeting. Until then, give Alison my love."

May 12, 2025

Jesse had been back on Sanibel Island for nearly two weeks before he felt up to going to the Monday Council meeting. He told Beverly, Alison, and Michael of the deal he struck with the regional militia at Fort Myers, and the need to sail to the Caymans. Now he needed to share details with the Council members. Beverly had shared the details of the pregnancy and he had gotten assurances from Dr. Wilson as well that both mother and child were doing extremely well. Dr. Wilson estimated due date as September 1, ironically close to Labor Day.

157

That would make the date of conception somewhere near the first of December, consistent with time they had shared on *Serenity*.

Beverly had deliberately not told Jesse anything about the attempted attack on her life. The serial killings this year had all the earmarks of random and opportunistic events. The close encounter with the killer had the odd and perverse effect of reverse psychology. Instead of feeling more frightened and insecure, Beverly actually felt the opposite. She had had her encounter with the madman and had escaped. It would not happen again; after all, lightning never strikes twice in the same location. Right? More likely she was feeling more secure because Jesse was home. Jesse was home, and that was all she needed, period.

Beverly and Jesse set a wedding date at long last. Neither wanted to wait very long but they could not decide whether to get married before or after sailing to the Grand Cayman's to pick up the gold demanded by the militia at Fort Myers. Complicating the decision was the insistence by Beverly that she accompany Jesse on the trip. She often did demure and concede to Jesse's wishes on many things, but not in this case. She insisted that she would accompany him on the dangerous journey. He insisted that she would not. Their argument raged well into the evening and nearly made them cancel their wedding plans. The next morning, they fell in love all over again, made love, made their apologies, and recommitted themselves one to another.

They decided on Sunday, June 9, as the date they would sail to the Grand Cayman's. This would give Jesse a full month to regain his strength, heal his injuries, and help guide Sanibel toward regaining a sustaining infrastructure.

The wedding date was set for two weeks after that, June 23. They started making a list of invitees. Beverly broke down and cried hard after she automatically put Marti Leinart on the list. She could not bear to mark through the name. She knew that Marti would be there in spirit.

. . . . .

The Monday Council meeting was now routinely set for 1 PM. This gave the members a chance to have lunch. The meetings went more smoothly when no one was "hangry", and in a hurry to raise their blood sugar. Jesse called the meeting to order promptly at 1 o'clock.

"The first order of business," began Jesse, "is to catch each other up on events of the last month. My news, as many of you already know, is that Jeffrey and I were detained and treated rather poorly in Fort Myers. They are, as you can imagine, still quite bitter about the massacre at the Caloosahatchee River. They extracted some teeth and fingernails from Jeffrey. All they took from me was my spleen."

Jesse looked at Jeffrey for confirmation. Jeffrey responded with a subtle nod.

"We did work out a deal for the electricity, and it is my understanding that it has been reliable recently. Fort Myers is demanding a hundred and twenty thousand dollars in gold bullion, and an increase in electronic bank credits from the $25,000 a month that we are paying currently to an exorbitant $60,000 a month. For this they will stop the arbitrary power outages and double our available kilowatt hours. With this additional power, however, we should be able to provide electricity to more than just the 40 or so homes and businesses that currently have it. Jeffrey, why don't you look into and suggest where, in addition to the community kitchen, Dr. Wilson's office, the Marina, your sheriff's department, the desalinization plant, the bank, and two or three restaurants that already have electricity, where else you would recommend we prioritize to receive power? We should be able to add another forty or fifty locations."

"Will do," replied Jeffrey. "And just so the rest of you know, Jesse pretty well left out the part where he was beaten within an inch of his life. It is probably going to be a month or more before he is ready to sail to the Caymans."

"That last part is true," confirmed Jesse, "but Dr. Wilson checked me over thoroughly, and I will be as good as new before too long. The tentative sail date is June 9th. The last part of the electricity discussion is to restate the obvious – we need to move rapidly to increase our renewable energy. We cannot stay dependent on the mainland for power. Let's move on to Sanibel's business. Jeffrey can you update us on the murders?"

"There is really not much to add," began Jeffrey. "Marti's death a month ago was all the more tragic because of how well we all knew her and

161

loved her. We are encouraging people to lock their doors because her death marks the third home invasion. People are also being encouraged to not be out alone after dark. We still have no description, no fingerprints or DNA, no motive or pattern, nothing. We only make the presumption that the killer is a male because of the strength and skill that is required, but there *are* women who could do this just as well. The victims have been younger and older, all female so far, some were relatively well-off, and on the other hand, some were homeless. I cannot find a pattern to any of it. My deputy, Russell, tried to make something out of a broken door windowpane at Marti's. I personally think the killer just got sloppy and failed to check to see if the door was locked. He obviously did not know Marti, at least not the way I and each of you did, or he would have known that she did not typically lock her doors. Our best hope at this point is that this bastard will make a mistake. When he does, we will get him."

Jeffrey looked around the table to see if there were any questions. He tightened his lips in an enigmatic expression of part-determination and part-frustration. Inwardly however, he was feeling smug that he could fail to discover that he was the serial killer and at the same time dissect clues that seemed to point away from him. What a wonderful mind game!

"Another thing Jeffrey failed to mention about our time in Fort Myers," Jesse announced anecdotally, "was that when he was allowed to fight back in a six on one matchup, he took out a half-dozen of their warriors. He put them out of commission without killing any of them. Otherwise they would never have let us go. I'm sure of it. But he sure got their respect." The room was duly impressed by Jesse's description, and Jesse was feeling good about supporting Jeffrey in his bid for the Sheriff's office. The Council members flashed glances of admiration and appreciation for their kung fu warrior hero.

Barefoot Chuck was the next to speak. "The fishing industry is doing very well for us. A lot of people are going out with purpose, not the typical touristy sport fishing. They found some good locations, and they're bringing in good hauls. We have been able to secure a delivery of gasoline and we are dedicating it to the boats. I don't think there are any cars on the island with internal combustion engines anyway.

"Except my Rubicon," said Michael.

"We've worked with other fishermen around here to designate some areas as off limits, to develop sustainable fish populations," continued Chuck, ignoring the interruption. "We've also imported some layer hens to supplement the chickens that were already on the island, which was not many. We also have some other breeds that are for meat production and most of the roosters are with that group. We have a smaller area set aside for roosters and the egg laying hens to provide us with more layer hens. One interesting use we have discovered for the salvaged garage doors is to repurpose them as chicken coops. You would have to see it to believe it. Anyway we are, or soon will be, self-sufficient with regard to chicken and eggs. The produce should be coming to market in two or three weeks. We can quit using canned goods at that time and save them for a rainy day. The bottom line is, we are able to feed ourselves, and soon we may have enough of a surplus to begin to trade with the mainland."

"Good news, Chuck!" Jesse said with a quick smile. "The boat driver who brought me back suggested regular weekly ferry boats and the restart of trade. So... *good news*. Michael?"

"Not much news on the medical front. We're all glad and relieved to have Jesse back. Medical supplies have held up well enough. We are low on tetanus and morphine, but that's nationwide. I am not seeing anywhere near the volume on PTSD and emotional trauma from the invasion, but people are anxious and worried about the murders. I know Jeffrey's doing all that can be done, but we really need to catch this guy. Nothing else from me."

"Mercedes?"

"Parks and Recreation, as I call it, reports continued progress. Liz couldn't make it. She's teaching a pottery class. People are finding the stoneware cookware to be quite useful. That is her report for the week, now here's mine. We have divested the nurseries of the more exotic plants, and are starting to focus on native species, especially those that are also edible. We have greenhouse operations that are focusing on vegetables and fruit trees. I really think Sanibel is going to be better than it ever was."

"That's great news, Mercedes. I agree," said Jesse. "Bert?"

"The island water supplies are doing very well now that the electricity is on continuously. We plan to flush one of the wells in a month or two, but no hurry. All of the major potholes are repaired or filled in with landscaping. There was only minor damage from shelling at the elementary school, and we plan to offer all grades in that building come September. I think there may be three or four dozen children on the island, but Mrs. Cochran might have a more accurate account with her census data. The tennis court at the school was cratered by a shell, and we plan to fill the hole with water and teach aquaponics to the children. I have a small team working with me now, and everything seems to be relatively smooth. That's it."

"Good, Bert, thanks," said Jesse. "Last but not least, Lucy? Anything to share with us?"

"I have an update on the census, Jesse. We're up to 687 known souls on the island. Forty-six of those are children under the age of eighteen."

Jesse and the others were silent, waiting for Lucy to continue. When they looked at her, she looked back and nodded. That was all she had to say. Jesse finally spoke, "Alright, then, I guess we're finished unless someone has a new problem or action plan they would like to discuss."

The room was quiet, then Mercedes said, "We are glad you are back, Jesse. We missed you and we were worried."

"Thanks, Mercedes," acknowledged Jesse. "I am more than a little glad to be back home. Meeting adjourned. See you next week. By the way, on a personal note, Beverly and I have set the date. You are all invited, of course. It's June 23rd, so save the date. We will be sending out invitations. We wanted to wait until we got back from the Caymans with the gold bullion. I need someone to talk her out of going with me. The last time I left the island, it wasn't any fun, but she is insisting on going."

Good to know, thought Jeffrey Rogers as the meeting broke up. *It would be better to let them get the gold to those scumbags in Fort Myers. Dependable electricity serves me as well. After that, I can take care of the blissful couple.*

.   .   .   .   .

167

It was a lovely spring day in Tennessee. Greg Johnston and Jennifer Marin were biking along a shady country road flanked by the woodlands of middle Tennessee. Wildflowers dotted their path. The shade and the breeze were in perfect counterpoint to the muggy heat. Even at only a moderate speed, the wind and the tire noise drowned out the sounds of the water splashing from rock to rock in the branch that kept them company alongside the road. They were going to visit the elephants. It used to be that no one saw the elephants except those who fed them. The Elephant Sanctuary in Tennessee was still the nation's largest, but it could not survive the economic collapse any more than any other entity. The donors who funded the foundation that fed the massive appetites had their limits. The sanctuary still functioned but the rules were gone, along with most of the staff.

The elephant sanctuary near Hohenwald was a favorite retreat and daytrip. If they did leave The Farm, they would very much miss seeing the elephants. They knew many of them by name.

The farmers had been generous with their reserves of hay, but who knows how long they could maintain their generosity given the challenges that

168

threatened their crops. Generations of elephants had taught the magnificent creatures a resourceful adaptation. Additionally, it was their way – the way of all wild things – to survive in the wild.

Jennifer and Greg slowed their bikes into a small clearing between the road and the creek. They left their bikes leaning against trees, and made their way along the creek bank, deeper into the deeply shaded and still forest. As they turned yet another bend, the creek got wider. A few more steps and it was wider still, forming a magical place – a deep pool brimming with trout and ringed by a rare patch of old growth forest. On the other side of the water stood their favorite elephants. The elephants knew them as well and made no attempt to leave. They rarely knew human companionship. Since the time when they were each retired from zoos and circuses, their human caregivers at the sanctuary were careful to "protect" them from human contacts. They had performed for their entire career; now they could spend their remaining time with other elephants in the wild. They formed bonds with friends, elephants of similar advanced age.

"This seems like a fine spot for a picnic," suggested Greg.

"It certainly does," agreed Jennifer.

Out of respect for the quiet of the forest, broken sweetly by songbirds and the soft utterances of the elephants, Greg and Jennifer slowly and deliberately went about the business of laying out the ground cloth, and sharing the small meal of cheese sandwiches and an apple. They shared a thermos of spring water, tasty with minerals, and it was as cool as it was when it came out of the pipe that was tapped long ago into the limestone hillside.

As the shadows grew longer, and the mosquitoes made their presence known, Greg and Jennifer said goodbye to their elephant friends who seemed in no hurry to leave. They made their way slowly up the creekside path to the small clearing where their bicycles stood loyally waiting. The ride home was slower, sadder somehow. There was a feeling of loss. There was a sense of disappointment, as if they had let down someone or something beyond themselves with their decision to leave The Farm.

.   .   .   .   .

May 27, 2025

It was raining softly. That should present no obstacle to Jeffrey. The moon was new and the night was black. He chose a large tall pine. He was wearing the steel footwear with spikes projecting from his soles, and he had a sturdy nylon rope that went from one hand around the tree to the other hand. With practiced agility and the deer stand strapped to his back, Jeffrey climbed the Australian pine rapidly, and secured his perch roughly 25 feet above the ground. He did not expect to be spotted, but if he were, then his alter ego, the sheriff, had a very plausible explanation. He was, of course, watching for any suspicious activity that would help him catch the serial killer. Meanwhile Jeffrey Rogers

171

watched and waited. Someone who would not spot him in the tree would come along the isolated path, if not soon, then eventually. Jeffrey would enjoy the wait.

Later that morning Jeffrey walked into the office on his way to bed. He kept a change of clothes there as well as in his condo. He was cold and wet from the rain which had gotten steadily stronger. He went straight to the showers. The warmth would be welcome.

Deputy Russell McGee offered coffee which Sheriff Rogers declined. He then offered, not for the first time, to take the more demanding night shift, which the sheriff again declined. No, the schedules were precisely as Rogers wanted them. But right this minute, he was scheduled to sleep.

Russell McGee holstered his firearm and left to make his morning rounds. The patrolling had become too routine, he mused.

He began to think in terms of What Would Sherlock Do? *When you eliminate everything and everyone that could not be responsible for the murders, then that which remains must be the source, no matter how unlikely.*

Lucy opened her door to Russell only after careful appraisal. "Sorry for the wait," she offered.

"No explanation needed," said Russell. "May I come in?"

"Yes, Russell. Of course."

As Sheriff John Cochran's widow, Lucy was well-trained in the use of firearms. Russell had no doubt that Lucy would not hesitate to use what ever she had in the hand that was behind her back.

"How goes the investigation?" she asked. "That is what I want to talk about," said Russell. "I know you have a rough census for Sanibel. How many are on the list now?"

"We've found a few more people to add this week, including Henry Farber, Sanibel's former mayor. The total is now 695."

"Where has Henry Farber been hiding out?" asked the deputy, newly suspicious of the man. "And can I get a list of names, so I can start eliminating everyone with solid alibis. There should be only 300 or so adult males. I will start with those."

"Smart thinking, Deputy." Lucy complimented. "Using the process of elimination to

173

narrow the focus sounds like something John would have done."

"High praise coming from you, Mrs. Cochran."

"And you wouldn't believe where we found Henry. Ask him where he's been when you see him."

June 10, 2025

It was after midnight and the torrents of rain came now in fierce and powerful gusts of wind. Everything was threatened. Tropical storm Denise rapidly became *Hurricane* Denise, with landfall expected within a few hours near Cape Coral. Jesse was desperate, frantically trying to save his precious sailboat *Serenity*.

Early yesterday he and Beverly wisely canceled their planned trip to the Cayman islands. They knew a storm was coming, but they did not yet know that it was going to be a category three or four hurricane. There was no hardware store from which to purchase plywood on Sanibel. Beverly recalled a stack of plywood boards in a storage room at the

175

house. When Jesse went to see what they had, he was thrilled and relieved to find 5/8-inch marine grade plywood cut to the size of the windows and marked accordingly – north one, north two, east one, and so forth. Jesse had never been more grateful to Brady Chapman that he was at that moment. After boarding the windows and sandbagging the garage and patio doors, after selecting food for coolers and filling the containers and bathtub with water, after storing the patio furniture, bicycles, and anything else with the liability of becoming flying debris, Jesse and Beverly had turned their attention to *Serenity*.

Jesse was known for his calm and even demeanor. It was highly uncharacteristic for him to be so anxiety ridden, but as the wind increased in intensity and as the rain stung like fire ants, every moment and everywhere, his desperation grew. Jesse was accustomed to problem solving, and he was good at it. That is what made it all the more difficult to accept that he could not save his beloved boat.

The wind was one challenge. Moored in the canal near their house, the small yacht could be secured with ropes to the wooden pilings on both sides of the canal. At the very least this measure would prevent the winds, expected to reach 150 mph or more, from bashing the boat repeatedly on the concrete surrounding the canals. It would, however, do nothing to prevent pieces of houses and trees from crashing down on *Serenity*.

The real threat from all hurricanes is the storm surge. The storm surge from hurricane Denise threatened to be 10 feet or higher. Add to that the high tide, the effect of the gravitational pull of the moon, and Sanibel was facing unprecedented flooding. The lines that secured *Serenity*, that kept her buoyant and safe, might also serve to drag her underwater if the storm surge was high enough. Jesse could not have it both ways. If the lines were long enough to let serenity stay afloat despite the flooding, then they would be too long to keep her from repeatedly crashing against her surroundings. Jesse had to limit the length of the lines that secured *Serenity*. If she sunk, if she went under, then he could salvage her. If she were broken into pieces, there would be nothing he could do to get her back. The frustration that went with Jesse's loss of control, his inability to protect *Serenity*, had generated an anxious discomfort like none he had ever

177

experienced. He could only imagine the level of panic he would feel if he were unable to protect Beverly and the baby in a similar manner. There was nothing left to do in the black of night, and the pelting rain and gale force winds, but to go home and hunker down. Hurricane Denise was on her way.

There was nothing romantic or exciting about their arduous journey from *Serenity* across a neighbor's yard, across a narrow street, another 50 yards along the concrete driveway, and finally to the right of the house and through a door where Alison and Michael were waiting for them. Alison and Michael's house was beachfront. And although it was sturdy, constructed from the best materials, it was hugely vulnerable. Although it was not common to have a vehicle on Sanibel, Michael still had his Rubicon. Alderman's troops had driven away with most of the cars on the island – many of them high end luxury models. Michael had been allowed to keep his Jeep as a concession and recognition of his indiscriminate service to the wounded, including Alderman's troops. Michael had driven the Rubicon and parked it for security in

Jesse and Beverly's garage. If only protecting *Serenity* was that easy.

Jesse began to wonder if they had waited too late to start the short trip back home. Beverly's pregnancy was a challenge to her balance and stamina under ordinary circumstances. The powerful wind gusts that swelled without warning had twice caused her to lose her footing. There was very little traction on either the waterlogged lawn of the neighbor or the rain slick asphalt of Beach Drive.

Jesse had kept a length of rope. They decided it would be best if they each tie one end around their waists. As they held each other tight they ran for the house. The rope did them no good as the wind blew them off their feet and sent them sailing east on Beach Drive. They approached a metal road sign, and with feet slipping and sliding, Jesse pushed Beverly to one side of it as he claimed the other. The metal pole caught the rope, and as the gust subsided, Jesse and Beverly strained against the wind, clothing drenched and flapping, two steps forward and one slide back until they reached the windbreak of their house. They pushed through the door, closed it, and collapsed in exhaustion. Michael and Alison ran to them, helped them up, and walked

179

them to their bedroom where they could towel dry and change into dry clothing.

The four friends then gathered in the living room to wait out the storm. As the wind howled like a runaway freight train, they discussed which of the locations in the house they should designate as their "safe room". Brady had used an interior room for his secured electronic communications. The door resembled that of a bank vault but without the combination locks and levers or the giant wheel that resembled the steering wheel of a sailing vessel. That room was chosen as their designated "safe room" if one became necessary.

Another feature was a pull-down folding ladder that led to the attic. If the storm surge flooded the interior of the house, it might be necessary to retreat to the space with the insulation and the rafters. Jesse also considered taking a chainsaw with him in case they needed to get out on the roof.

The wind continued to howl. None of them slept despite their exhaustion. They felt a ground shaking event – a crackle followed by a deep "thud" – that suggested a large tree had fallen nearby. Then there was another, and another. Sanibel was being littered with the shallow rooted Australian Pines –

the invasive species that had been thoughtlessly brought in to decorate Periwinkle well over a century before.

The wind howled on and on. There was no more conversation as the four dozed lightly from sheer exhaustion. They were startled awake by a loud sharp crash that shook the room. Something large – housing debris, perhaps part of a roof – had hit their house traveling well over 100 mph. They got up to inspect the western walls with flashlights. They saw no signs of water leakage, at least not yet. They became aware of numerous other strikes that the house was taking. Not as severe as the crash that woke them, but numerous peltings, nevertheless.

Jesse was worried. What chance did *Serenity* have of surviving a storm of this magnitude? Indeed, what chance did Sanibel have? Sanibel was a barrier island, the purpose of which was to absorb the brunt of the storm. Buildings, trees, crops and the rest of man's follies were expected to be impermanent. Man makes plans, and God laughs. This was a proverb as true as it was ancient.

The wind howled as fiercely as ever. Jesse had no idea of the time. He made his way to the garage and looked out the small horizontal windows. It was dark out. The time passed with interminable hesitation. It was as if nothing good could come from this, so what was the hurry? Why not run everything in slow motion? World without end. Amen.

Jesse sat in the middle of the couch. Beverly and her gravid abdomen cuddled on his left. Alison leaned on his right side. The three were sound asleep when Michael gently shook Jesse shoulder.

"I think it is starting to let up," said Michael.

Jesse opened his eyes and listened. The sounds of wind and debris were much fainter. He gently extricated himself from the women, who fell over slowly toward each other. Michael and Jesse tucked their legs up under them on the couch. Beams from their flashlights guided them to the garage. The boarded house remained pitch black, but there was a gloomy gray glow from the garage windows.

When they looked out, they could not believe what they were seeing. "It is far worse than the shelling from Alderman's troops," said Michael. "This is an unmitigated disaster."

Jesse reached up and pulled the garage door lever that attached it to the mechanical opener. Once freed, the door could be lifted manually. The two men stepped outside. It was raining and the wind was brisk and steady. It was not going to knock you down, but it still made walking treacherous. There was debris everywhere. Australian Pines, some nearly 100 feet tall, littered the grounds. Large sections of decking, siding, and roofing collected in piles. One had to look no further to understand that Sanibel had been destroyed by the storm. The storm surge had come and gone, but the erosion and damage from the flooding was evident.

"How do you think Alison's house did?" asked Jesse.

"I am about to find out," said Michael. He climbed into the Rubicon and slowly backed it into the driveway. Maneuvering sometimes over and sometimes around the limbs and pieces of houses, Michael worked his way towards Alison's beach house.

Jesse went around the house to inspect for damage and especially to see what caused the loud crash during the night. It was clear as he turned the corner. A section of someone's roof had come to a stop against the stucco of their western wall. The wall had held its ground, and the damage was cosmetic.

Jesse turned south, climbing around the debris on Beach Drive. *Serenity* was as he left her, secured by her moorings and still afloat. She was battered and cluttered by limbs and roofing materials, but the damage, once again, was superficial and cosmetic. *Serenity* would sail again, weather permitting.

Jesse worked his way through the soggy piles of trash. When he got back, the Rubicon was still gone, but the women were up and preparing something to eat by flashlight. Jesse got a crowbar and removed some of the plywood coverings from the key windows. Light flooded the interior of the house. It was much appreciated.

The women looked out the windows. They were prepared for storm damage, but they were not prepared for the utter devastation they now beheld.

Jesse came inside and set the crowbar on a table in the garage. As he entered the kitchen, Alison asked about Michael.

"He took the Jeep to check on your place," said Jesse. "With all the downed trees, he may have to park it and walk. This house seems to have come

184

through the storm pretty well from what I can tell. We stopped a neighbor's roof, but the damage to us does not seem structural. *Serenity* seems basically okay, too."

"How much can you tell about Sanibel?" asked Beverly.

"I've never seen anything like it," replied Jesse. "I thought things were bad after that army had been here. In the past we would have needed heavy equipment, teams of municipal workers, and probably some kind of federal aid in order to rebuild. There's only about 700 of us left on Sanibel, and after this I suspect at least half of those will leave. It is bleak. And just when we were starting to get back on our feet. I am sure the crops are gone, and the greenhouses, and the trees, and a lot of buildings," his voice trailed off.

Jesse sat down hard in a chair. Beverly came to him but didn't know what to say. She sat partly on the arm of the chair and partly on his knee, leaned in and pulled his head to her chest. There were no words.

The three ate lunch in silence. Later they went outside through the garage. Jesse used the crowbar to remove the remaining plywood, then carried the plywood and the sandbags to the storage room where they initially found them. They swept the debris from the patio and carried out the patio furniture from the garage. The wind was still stiff, but it carried a fresh salt spray and it felt good in the muggy heat. There was still no sign of Michael.

In the distance a chainsaw buzzed. Someone was working their way out of their cage of fallen trees. Was it a sign of hope that people could get up off the map twice? Or was it a sign of desperation?

Jesse started his own engine, a portable generator. He connected it to the breaker box that had been modified for emergency generator use. It ran a few essential circuits in the house, primarily for the freezer and the kitchen circuits. Then he went back out to the patio where the women were sitting on dry cushions. The rain had stopped, but the wind would persist for days. There were birdsongs in the distance, but it seemed like a token effort, not the cheerful stuff of a new dawn, a new day, a new life.

Beverly said to him, "I will get us cheese if you will pick a wine."

"You can't have wine," Jesse said."

"You're right," she said meekly. She held her pregnant abdomen with both hands, and

186

repositioned herself in the chair, trying to work through some of the stiffness from the awkward sleep during the storm. "But you two can. Alison?"

"Yes, thank you. That would be appreciated."

Jesse left to pick a bottle of wine while Beverly retrieved a tray of cheese and apples. They heard a third engine in the neighborhood – the unmistakable deep throated whine of Michael's Rubicon. Jesse went back for a third glass.

As Michael approached the group, Beverly asked, "How is the house?"

"I never got there," replied Michael wearily. "There were bodies. I saw two. Some were injured and I did what I could for them without medicine or equipment. I did manage to set a broken arm with found materials. I used to keep a bag in the Jeep. I need to start doing that again."

"Jesse," Michael continued, "I doubt my office survived the hit, not given what I have seen so far. The first priority needs to be to send out search and rescue teams. We will need to designate the library or the City Hall as a triage center. Some cases we can handle locally but others we will need to ferry to the hospital in Fort Myers. I know how badly they treated you there, and I am sure that they will be overwhelmed as it is, but lives are on the line. We have no other choice."

Jesse and Michael set out on foot. It would take many days before the main roads were passable due to the large number of fallen trees. It was nearly an hour before they reached the town hall. People were already gathering. Some had brought wounded neighbors, and Michael went straight to work attending to them.

Jesse got busy organizing search teams and sending them to specific locations. It was important to search as much of the island as possible before dark. Several women were assisting Michael, serving as nurses and bandaging minor wounds. Several of the Council members were there, and Jesse assigned Barefoot Chuck the chore of creating a ferry service to Fort Myers. It would be first light tomorrow before he would know if the seas had settled down enough to allow safe passage.

Just over a year-and-a-half after the invaders pulled out, Sanibel was beginning its second major effort at recovery. People were less certain of success this time around.

. . . . .

Fernando Lopez was sitting in a cushioned Adirondack style chair reading a book he had recently selected from the community library at The Farm. The room in which he was sitting was one of a number of community spaces that were as unique and artful as they were utilitarian. The centerpiece was a giant fireplace that resembled a cartoonish giant figure from the Easter Islands. The firebox was an enormous mouth that would happily eat the wood it was fed during the winter months. The enormous eyes could literally breathe through their eyelids like a master Yogi, such was the design of the ventilator system that circulated masonry heat back into the room.

Fernando was the most satisfied of the trio that had journeyed from Sanibel to The Farm. He, too, was concerned about the downturn in viability and the shrinking population, but he remained optimistic, or at least hopeful. From Gaskin's original 320 San Francisco hippies to a peak of 1500 residents, the population of The Farm had stabilized at roughly 180 men, women, and children. Another twenty or so churned as visitors and seekers, searching for answers to questions that they could not yet find the right words to properly ask.

Lost in his reverie, sometimes reading sometimes daydreaming, Fernando stirred himself to wakefulness when Greg and Jennifer came in and sat down. He was pleased to see them. They had been keeping to themselves more in recent weeks, and it felt good to have the gang back together. "How are the elephants?" Fernando asked.

"Good, I suppose," replied Jennifer, "but that's not where we were today."

"There wasn't much to do in the fields, so we went for a bike ride. We are getting to know the countryside quite well," Greg added. The irony lost on Fernando was that much of the discussion between Greg and Jennifer centered on leaving The Farm for the Gulf Coast if not a return to Sanibel. It was time to share the notion with Fernando. "Go with us," Greg pleaded.

"I don't know," said Fernando. "Let me consider it a while. I want to stay here at least until the thirteenth anniversary remembrance that they are organizing for July 1."

"The anniversary of Steven Gaskin's death," acknowledged Jennifer.

"Yes," replied Fernando. "The more I learn about him, and his teachings, the more I realize how unique and special the man was."

"I am sorry to say that I've been here nearly two years, and I know very little about the man who founded this place," said Jennifer. "Tell me some of the highlights."

"Okay. There have been a number of biographies written since his death in 2014, but I can give you a little summary," offered Fernando. "He was born into a long line of freethinkers and activists. He was a Korean War Marine Corps combat veteran who morphed into a San Francisco hippy philosopher who taught college English. In the early 70s he and his followers decided that San Francisco had gotten too decadent, so they moved to Tennessee, bought 1000 acres, and established this collective they called the Black Swan Farm. Mostly he was on the spiritual quest, but that included vegetarian self-sufficiency as well as acid trips. He once said, 'It's easier to be God than it is to find God.' He also said, 'I'm a teacher not a leader. If you lose your leader you might lose your way, but if you lose

191

your teacher and you learned what was taught, then there's a chance you can still find your way.' Or something like that. He was also a huge supporter of the Constitution. He taught that it protected not only freedom of religion, but freedom from religion. He said that he considered any attempt to take this country over in the name of religion was as repugnant as having it taken over by fascism or communism. There was a lot to admire in this man. He was a good man who tried to walk the walk, not just talk the talk. He didn't try to coerce anybody to follow him so much as he did the right thing himself, and others saw that and followed his example. He was one heady mix of spirituality, ecology, freedom, and sustainability. That's about all I know."

"Wow," said Jennifer admiringly. "I wish I had been around to meet him."

"Yeah, me too," added Greg. It was Fernando's soliloquy, so he kept it to himself that it was his (Greg's) idea to travel to The Farm in the first place. "So, maybe a month from now, do you think you might want to go south with us, or stick around here?"

"Like I said," Fernando responded, "let me think on it. I think I may stay put, at least for another year or two. I like the vibe here."

June 23, 2025

Island hardships, critical shortages of electricity and water, food supplies, and just getting from one place to another had become critical issues on Sanibel. The death toll was a staggering thirty-seven people. Of the 660 islanders left alive, perhaps 100 packed what meager possessions they could carry and shuttled to the mainland to begin a nomadic existence. Unfortunately, this self-selected lot was among the more able-bodied individuals on the island. Those who remained were too invested in scrounging for necessities to be involved in helping the larger community dig out. This time

194

there was precious little in the way of organized community cleanup. None of this, however, could prevent Jesse and Beverly from following through with their appointed nuptials. Their wedding day was happening as scheduled.

With Alison as the maid of honor and Michael as Jesse's best man, the hustle and bustle of the pre-matrimonial preparations was as chaotic as ever. Jesse and Beverly had spent the weeks following hurricane Denise cleaning the debris from their property and preparing the house for the reception. The wedding itself was to take place in the foyer of the library. It was the nicest of Sanibel's municipal structures, and it escaped the hurricane relatively unscathed. Over 100 friends and neighbors attended the wedding. It was exactly the kind of positive event that the community was desperately needing.

The ceremony itself was charming. The bride and groom had penned the words themselves. The officiant was a surprise to many. Barefoot Chuck was ordained as a minister by the Universal Life Church many decades ago, and true to the affectation that earned him his name, he wore neither shoes nor socks.

195

Dearly beloved, we are gathered here today – in the presence of God, and in the company of those we love – to witness as these two beach bums – Beverly McMahan and Jesse O'Connell – join their lives together in Holy Matrimony, the most sacred of relationships. Because you have known and loved them as individuals, you have been invited to share in the joyous moment as they join their lives together as one, and then go eat all of their food.

This is the time which you have chosen to become husband and wife. We are here not only to witness your commitment to each other, but to wish you both every happiness in your future life together. If anyone has reason why these two should not be so joined, let him speak now, or forever hold his peace. C'mon... anyone. Really?

Before you are joined in marriage in my presence and in the presence of these, your family, friends and witnesses, I am to remind you of the solemn and enduring nature of the

196

relationship into which you are about to enter.

Do you Jesse O'Connell take Beverly McMahan to be your first mate and lawfully wedded wife? From this day forward, to have and to hold, forsaking all others, for better or for worse, for richer and poorer, in sickness and health, to love and cherish for so long as you both shall live? Also, you can do your share of the dish washing.

Jesse: "I do."

And do you Beverly McMahan take Jesse O'Connell to be the captain of your ship and your lawfully wedded husband? From this day forward, to have and to hold, forsaking all others, for better and for worse, for richer and poorer, in sickness and health, to love and cherish for so long as you both shall live? Also, you should learn to cook.

Beverly: "I do."

Jesse, what token of your devotion do you offer your beloved? Jesse retrieved the rings from

Michael and Alison, and handed them to Barefoot Chuck.

May these rings be blessed as the symbol of this affectionate union. These two lives are now joined in one unbroken circle -- a sign that life, happiness, and love have no beginning and no end. A wedding ring represents eternal love and commitment.

Barefoot Chuck handed one of the rings to Jesse and said, "Jesse O'Connell, in placing this ring on Beverly McMahan's finger, repeat after me:

'I give you this ring as pledge of my love, and as the symbol of our unity.' At which time Jesse repeated the words and placed the ring on Beverly's finger.

Barefoot Chuck handed the other ring to Beverly and said, "Beverly McMahan, in placing this ring on Jesse O'Connell's finger, repeat after me:

'I give you this ring as the pledge of my love and as the symbol of our unity.'

Beverly did as instructed.

Barefoot Chuck continued. "Inasmuch as Beverly McMahan and Jesse O'Connell have consented together in marriage before this company; have pledged their faith and declared their unity by each giving and receiving a ring -- and are now joined in mutual esteem and devotion, by the authority vested in me by the Universal Life Church and the State of Florida, pronounce that they are husband and wife. What God hath here joined together, let no one set asunder. You may kiss the bride, proclaiming joy to the entire world.

Beverly was radiant with tears of joy. Jesse was beaming with pride and happiness. The joy and love were infectious, and everyone attending felt deeper love for those close to them than they had been able to feel in a long time.

Jeffrey came up to the newlyweds and was effusive in his praise and happiness. Years of political dealings in the NSA had made Jeffrey a highly accomplished diplomat and sycophant. Periods of undercover activity had honed his acting ability in settings where believability was a life or death matter. Jesse was not in the least interested or focused on Jeffrey's motives, so he innocently welcomed and internalized Jeffrey's kind wishes as being sincere. He and Beverly were lambs awaiting the slaughter, as far as Jeffrey was concerned. Why not tell them something nice in the lead up?

.   .   .   .   .

Some bicycled and some walked, but everyone came to Beverly and Jesse's for the reception. Bowls of nonalcoholic fruit punch were set out on a patio tables. Many of their friends had contributed to the spread of food that included charcoal grilled vegetables, and fruits, local fish, deviled eggs, and cheeses. All of the chickens on the island were for breeding and eggs, so they were not fully represented at the banquet. Given the scarcity of food and the absence of electricity following Hurricane Denise, it may not have been everything that Beverly and Jesse would have wished for, but it was more than anyone had expected, and everyone was grateful for the feast.

More than the food, what made the events so special for so many was the opportunity to feel good about life again. The party went into the late afternoon when, with Michael's help, the house was cleared of the guests and locked as the last of the food was set out on the patio.

Michael the co-conspirator distracted the crowd by bringing out his guitar and leading a boisterous sing-along while Jesse and Beverly snuck away, noticed only by Jeffrey. They rode their bikes east toward the Port of Sanibel.

"I have a surprise for us," said Jesse with childlike excitement.

Beverly smiled widely from the glow of the day and the anticipation of Jesse surprise. As they approached the dock, she could see *Serenity*. She knew the surprise. Jesse had planned for a getaway honeymoon at sea. It would be time alone together, away from the tragedies that had defined Sanibel, and would be romantically reminiscent of when they first met and fell in love. Alone with her man where they both would feel the most comfortable and safe, nothing could be more perfect.

That night at sea, with *Serenity* gently rocked by the Gulf's calming waves and currents, Jesse and Beverly made love that was warm and tender, slow and deep, wet and wonderful, despite her advancing pregnancy. They slept and made love again. They made love again and slept some more. Occasionally they would come up for air. From *Serenity's* cockpit they could see the distant islands of Sanibel, Captiva, North Captiva, and a few points on the mainland. It looked perfect, unblemished, as beautiful as ever.

The newlyweds pledged their love, their adoration, their unending devotion. They used words of such intense feeling, that they would have been embarrassed for Barefoot Chuck to pronounce them to the assembled wedding guests. But in the end, they needed no words, no longing looks of love, no everlasting melting embraces; for what they experienced was a transcendent love that exploded with an indescribable depth of emotion. If they *could* have merged into one spiritual being, then it would have happened, and the result would have been pure light, brighter than the sun itself, and pure heat, hotter than lightning. Their love was love itself.

Book Two

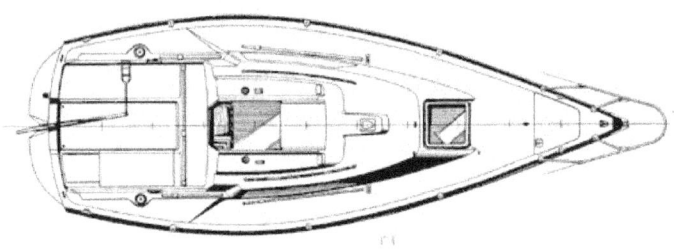

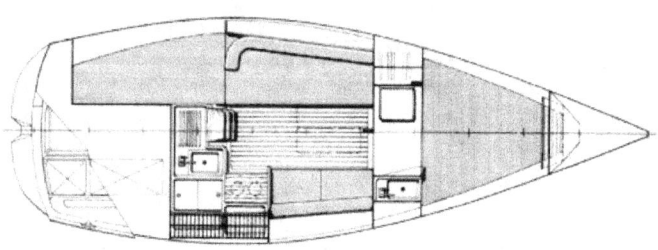

204

July 1, 2025

Freshly back from his honeymoon, Jesse had a spring to his step and a *joi de vivre* that the others could not match. He and Beverly had totally dismissed the tragedies of Sanibel, from the feuding with the mainland to the aftermath of the hurricane. Beverly and he had been able to focus so completely on each other to the exclusion of all else that it had been cathartic. Despite this afterglow, Jesse was indeed back, it was Monday, and there was much to get accomplished at the Monday Counsel meeting.

Jesse called the group to order at 1 o'clock. Most of the discussion centered on the slow progress that was being made in the wake of the disastrous

205

hurricane. There was no qualified lineman on Sanibel, so the Council had budgeted to pay someone from the mainland to come help repair the downed power lines. That work had started, and some power had already been restored. The homes of the various council members had electricity, as did Dr. Wilson's office, the community kitchen, the marina, and the municipal buildings.

The reports given by the various members revealed slow progress in many areas. Fewer people had volunteered to deal with the fallen Australian Pines, partly because so many were focused on repairing their own homes, or if repairs were not feasible, finding new places to live. The other reason discouraging people from volunteering was the sheer enormity of the task. Hurricane Denise had toppled the majority of the island's Australian Pines. Many others were broken off, snapped like twigs at various heights. The jagged landscape stood in grotesque contrast to the beauty of Sanibel that was now relegated to memory.

The crops had not been totally destroyed. The corn was gone. The tomato plants were damaged but would come back. The field crops from cucumbers and squash to watermelon and

206

cantaloupe were largely undamaged. The greenhouses were destroyed, but were already being replaced. Water was flowing and, indeed, was the one essential service that had not undergone interruption. The backup generators had worked beautifully, and the reverse osmosis plant had been the first to have power restored from the mainland.

Jesse announced that he and Beverly would be leaving today for the Cayman Islands in order to retrieve the gold demanded by the militia at Fort Myers. He reminded the Council members that the deadline for payment was the first of August, and that was just a month away. He said it was difficult to estimate how long the trip would take. The major variable was prevailing winds. There might be days when he made little progress if he were to become stuck in an area of calm winds. He estimated that he could average five nautical miles per hour, and he hoped to travel fifty or sixty miles per day. Jesse was allowing ten days to travel the 500 miles at sea, a day or two to conduct business, and another ten days to travel back to Sanibel. There was little room for error.

More business was discussed, the logistics of survival, but Jesse found it difficult to focus. The slow progress after the hurricane worried him. The health of the community that was necessary for determined and sustained efforts at rebuilding was disappearing.

He told the group that Sanibel was in good hands with them at the helm, and he had some thoughts. "As you know, I am a philosopher, and this is what I see happening on Sanibel. This is a hard, exhausting time, but it's also a pivot point. In periods of tumult and confusion many people *lose faith* in systems of change, like we are offering. We have to have the open exchange of views that is the essence of liberalism in the classical Enlightenment sense. We need to gather at the square. People are motivated by both self-interest and a yearning desire to lead a morally meaningful life, which is why liberalism has to be supplemented with the morality of personalism. Personalism is the belief that at the heart of any just society, there is an earnest and ongoing effort to see the full depth, dignity, and complexity of each human person. Personalism judges each social arrangement by how well it fosters the kind of relationships that enhance the full complexity and depth of each soul. This awful year will be somewhat redeemed if we can end it with a sense of this kind of common morality, and if we can begin the hard work of rebuilding our island to be in line with it."

Jesse took his leave to allow the Council to finish its meeting. He said his goodbyes all around, and the Council members wished him a safe and speedy voyage. He left to finish stocking *Serenity* with the provisions necessary for the journey. He wondered if sixty meals would be enough, especially since one of the travelers would be eating for two. When he factored in the potential for delay due to calm winds, he decided that it would not be enough. He would stock *Serenity* with additional provisions, he was hoping for good fishing along the way.

"What the fuck was that?" exclaimed Chuck after a stunned silence followed Jesse's departure.

"That's Jesse..." said Lucy Cochran.

"That's Jesse," Michael echoed Lucy. "Jesse gotta be Jesse."

"Meeting adjourned," declared Barefoot Chuck abruptly. No one spoke as they filed out of the library.

.   .   .   .   .

The Farm was buzzing with excitement over the events scheduled for the remembrance celebration on the 11-year anniversary of Stephen Gastin's death.

Fernando decided to stay.

"I can be a hermit," he had told them. "Or a Monk; an aesthetic; or a Gnostic. The Land will provide."

The Farm was clearly a haven for seekers, mystics, and those on a spiritual quest. Fernando was home.

.　　.　　.　　.　　.

July 14, 2025

Serenity, now at anchor, was bobbing to gentle gulf waves. Jesse was atop the boat, lying on his back looking at the stars. The curve of the fiberglass roof slightly hyperextended Jesse's spine, and the rocking of the waves was like heaven to his weary muscles, still healing from the mainland beatings.

The half-moon was low in the sky. The sky Jesse was immersed in was a deep clear black overlain with a rich tapestry of stars. Light pollution was cured by the economic and infrastructure collapses. But Jesse had no thoughts of recent happenings, rather he was gazing at and mindful of the universe – the vast, infinite, inexplicable universe. And mindful he was.

That is why he did not hear Beverly when she surfaced from below. Beverly had anticipated Jesse's sail from the island. She was *supposed* to go with him. After he had snuck out that night, she struck out with go bags at the ready and beat him to *Serenity* in barely enough time to hide.

They were well out to sea before Beverly revealed herself, and so it began. Their first real fight since their marriage was heated.

She wasn't about to let him do this alone, especially after the mainland vigilantes. And *he* wanted to take *her* back. For her to come was dangerous, and not just because of the pregnancy.

Finally they came to a decision that she could come and they would get a bigger boat. Jesse knew a guy.

"What cha thinkin'?" asked Beverly as she climbed to the cabin roof.

"Not much." Jesse whispered as he transitioned to a conversational state.

"Oh," recognized Beverly. "Well, I guess that was the point, to not be thinking."

"Yeah," agreed Jesse, trailing off.

And they lay there, gazing up at the stars.

Beverly was quiet, not wanting to disrupt Jesse's contemplative state, his meditation, his peace.

She fell into her own reverie, drifting in her own thoughts and feelings, as *Serenity* rocked and drifted within the range of her anchor. After a long while and an alphabet soup of dreams, Beverly awoke and said, "How did things get so crazy?"

They lay in silence for a time. Jesse sat up. "Are you okay? Bad dream?"

"Yeah," she said softly. "I guess *so.*"

"Let's go in," he suggested.

.   .   .   .   .

The next few days were eventful. After a late morning start, they set the sails to take them down the coastline towards Naples. There was safety in staying in sight of land when the seas were full of gangs of pirates. After a day of sea travel, they stopped at a private dock, owned by Jesse's friend, Hugh Langman. As a fitting accoutrement to his gulf-side estate, Hugh had in his service a yacht, a fast one. And yes, of course they could take it to the Caymans, after all he wouldn't be here if... He just

213

might go too, but no, not for a week. He had that *thing*. But the boat was fully staffed with a good crew. "Have the lobster thermidor," he advised.

Hugh introduced Jesse and Beverly to Captain O'Reilly and a crew of four. They pushed off minutes after Hugh left. He had that "thing".

On the open sea they spotted ships on the horizon, pacing and trailing them.

"Pirates," said Captain O'Reilly, dryly.

"Will they attack us?" asked Jesse.

"Not on the way there," assured the captain. "Not while we're riding high."

.　　.　　.　　.　　.

That evening, well fed and pampered by the staff, Jesse and Beverly found themselves alone on deck, a warm sea breeze in their faces. He spoke first.

"I've been wanting to get away from video monitors so I could ask you something."

"Okay. Go for it."

"Well, it's just that we're going to be in port in the Caymans, and there will be ganja, and I was curious how you felt about that."

Beverly had been curious about his agenda, but now she was just quiet. After a short period of self-composure, she said, "I will tell you the truth, not what you want to hear. My brother was a heavy marijuana user, one of the twenty percent who get addicted. He was psychotic at times, paranoid. I am reminded of some bad times that I associate with marijuana, so I would just as soon not be around it."

"I get it. No problem." After a period of quiet, he added, "What about Cuban cigars?"

"You're kidding now, right? They can be smelly, but outside they're okay."

"Like after a sumptuous meal? On the stern of a borrowed yacht? Maybe with a stiff breeze and the ocean falling away behind us?"

"Yes, maybe just like that, and maybe on deck chairs." Beverly was getting up and heading aft.

Jesse asked the staff for some cigars and cognac as he rose to follow her.

215

    ·   ·   ·   ·   ·

In the bustle of the autonomous British territory that was the Grand Cayman, Jesse and Beverly were pulled by handmade linens and lace, and aromas of market. A leisurely espresso in a sidewalk café allowed for people watching and window shopping without having to get up.

Jesse and Beverly explored the Cayman Islands and liked what they saw. In less than a day they swam with the stingrays in Stingray City, then with the dolphins in Dolphin Cove. They strolled hand in hand along Seven Mile Beach. That evening they dined on bluefin tuna sashimi, some Argentinian beef, chocolate from Bernachon in Lyon, half a dozen local oysters and clams. Jesse had a P.B.R. in a can (for the clams and oysters), a glass of white and then a glass of red burgundy wine with everything else. Beverly sipped water.

On the veranda of their stateroom that evening, Beverly and Jesse shared their thoughts and dreams from earlier, when times were less complicated and their thoughts and dreams for when times will be simpler again. After a period of comfortable silence Beverly said, "Let's go to our room."

"Yes, let's do, responded Jesse, but you go on. I want to sit here a few more minutes."

Beverly smiled at him as she left. Jesse needed to be alone with his thoughts.

After a short while, Jesse stood and went to their room.

.   .   .   .   .

When the bank opened its doors promptly at 10 a.m. the next morning, several men and women stepped forward to greet Mr. and Mrs. O'Connell. The bank president, Mr. Cruz, was the most effusive.

"Welcome Mr. O'Connell," he said to Jesse, then turned to Beverly. "Welcome Mrs. O'Connell, though I knew you first as Beverly McMahan. You have each stored your valuables here with us and now you are married. Yes? You honor us by being here with us. How may we help you today?"

Jesse explained the need for the gold as war reparations, and in a way they were. As they were leaving with an armored truck, Mr. Cruz was heard saying, "I'm just glad they didn't take it all."

In truth it was nearly one fifth of their combined storehouse of gold. Despite the vast wealth accumulated by Beverly's hit man friend and benefactor, Jesse's fortune comprised the bulk of the gold stored there. Beverly would have to ask him where it all came from someday. Neither one of them was that interested in their gold-based fortune. It came in useful, obviously, on days like this day. It served a means to an end, but the things Jesse and Beverly valued lay in their love for each other and their love for their friends.

.   .   .   .   .

The trip back could have been eventful. The ship was lower in the water and that would attract attention. Jesse hired armed ships to escort them to Florida. The pirates wanted no part of an armed and trained protectorate. It was a smooth trip. Hugh happily accepted a bar of gold for his loan of the yacht. One of the escort ships stayed on to tow *Serenity* home to Sanibel where it would anchor. The majority of the gold was transferred to *Serenity* to be deposited into the treasury of Sanibel. Jesse's naval mercenaries went with him and Beverly in an armed vessel with $120,000 in gold bullion from the Caymans to meet with representatives of the mainland in the final step of the deal to have electric power restored to the island. There would be no further trouble. War reparations, Jesse had called it, though he knew there could never be sufficient reparations for man's cruelties.

August 3, 2027

Greg Johnston and Jennifer Marin left The Farm about 5 a.m. and planned to travel overland until 7 p.m. before finding a place to rest for the night. They had said their "good-byes", and after months of debating whether to leave, they were ready, even eager. The soft summer moon provided ample light as they walked briskly southward down Walker Road. They each carried a large backpack filled with those possessions they valued enough to bother to carry. Each had room for more but had all they needed. Drake Lane took them to highway 20 and that to Summertown and breakfast – fried eggs and bacon, biscuits and gravy at Dawn's Family Deli.

Venturing south again but with a hearty meal for the road, they crossed the Buffalo River, and would have taken it if it were flowing south rather than west. They walked at a brisk pace and made it down a deserted U.S. Hwy 43 to the Alabama state line by 5 or 6 o'clock. They carried nothing that told the time. It had been a long first day and they were discovering some forgotten muscles.

Greg and Jennifer wore to a halt in Anderson, by God, Alabama, where they began looking for shelter from the storm that was brewing. They made their way to the Joe Wheeler State Park, nestled on the north shore of the Tennessee River. As expected there were no park rangers or other state employees there. Not surprisingly, people had settled the rooms and cabins; modest accommodations now made splendid by an *ad hoc* intentional community. The public restrooms had *showers* Jennifer realized.

Jennifer and Greg approached slowly, respectfully, until they reached speaking distance. "May we approach?" asked Jennifer.

"Please do," replied Jessica, a woman near Jennifer's age, thin but fit.

221

As they walked toward the small group of people and the line of cabins, Jennifer continued, "We left The Farm this morning. We need a place to crash for the night. Then we will be on our way."

"You may certainly pitch camp here. You will be safe," said Jessica sweetly. "Sites on the golf course would be private for you."

Jennifer looked around at the rocky ground. "Thank you," she said. And continued her search for a campsite. "There is one more request if I may."

"What would that be? We have no food," said Jessica, less sweetly.

"Greg and I left The Farm this morning on our way to find family in Florida. We're pregnant and want to get married with family present. I know the cabins are fully occupied, but I was wondering if we could roll out our sleeping bag on somebody's wooden porch."

An older lady in the crowd was touched. "Oh, honey, of course you can. Shoot, you can have my bed. I'll take the couch."

"'Yes' to the porch. But 'No' to the bed. Thank you so much Ms…"

"Harriet."

"Well, thank you so very much, Ms. Harriet."

"Okay, child. You two follow me and we'll get you settled in."

Greg shouldered his bag and followed Jennifer who was following Harriet to her cabin. He was processing the bombshell that Jennifer was pregnant and hadn't told him. Maybe Greg wasn't the father. Maybe Jennifer made up the story. There's no family in Florida. He was processing hard and painfully while holding his composure. He was rooting for the last option. Jennifer and Greg both smiled shyly at Jessica as they passed. She had been nice, and that gave them hope for the journey to come. Greg called back to Jessica, "Hey, we know a place that plowed up their golf courses; turned them into vegetable gardens. I think that worked out well for them."

"Thanks," acknowledged Jessica. "We will look into that."

.   .   .   .   .

Alone and whispering on the quiet wooden porch, Jennifer and Greg listened to the night sounds atop their large wide sleeping bag. A breeze off the hillsides cooled the August night, and they were comfortable in light cotton.

"Are we pregnant?" whispered Greg.

"Sorry about that. Thanks for playing along," whispered Jennifer, and she snuggled up tight against him. "But we can't..."

"Best not," agreed Greg.

The next morning they graciously accepted the hard-boiled eggs they were given. They hit the road at dawn.

.   .   .   .   .

Beverly and Jesse had docked at the Sanibel Pier. Jesse would have preferred 'Tween Waters but conveyance to the southern end of the island was not assured. Their first encounter was with Barefoot Chuck. Chuck had been there when Jesse got back from his torture trip to the mainland. He was guarding the pier and directing the fishing initiative.

He sent the properly-equipped boats to the areas that had sustainable fishing waters. They had even acquired a shrimp boat, salvaged after the hurricane and repaired.

After saying their goodbyes to Barefoot Chuck, they were caught up enough on the local news. They headed home. Home! Home would be heaven. *There* would be peace.

Days of rest, sleep and love making did wonders for the newly-weds. They were ready to venture out after three days of time spent cocooning at home.

.   .   .   .   .

Michael Wilson had called for this gathering so that Sheriff Rogers could confer with him and Jesse on the murders' investigation. Jeffrey brought them up to date on the numbers, the seemingly randomness of the victims (but all women), the locales, the absence of evidence or clues. Tips are well-intentioned and all are investigated, but so far nothing. Jeffrey did not mention Deputy McCoy's strategy of eliminating everyone who failed to fit the pattern or had a good alibi, primarily because McCoy had not mentioned it to him.

.   .   .   .   .

Dr. Wilson and Alison got married.

"I do," replied Michael Wilson.

And do you, Alison Swanson, take this man, Michael Wilson, to be your lawful wedded husband? Do you promise to love and cherish him, in sickness and in health, for richer for poorer, for better for worse, and forsaking all others, keep yourself only unto him, for so long as you both shall live?"

"I do."

Jesse smiled, amused at his thought. He had considered whispering to Beverly *I do too*.

Later, above the soft murmurings of the throng of well-wishers filing out, Beverly pulled Jesse so that his ear was closer to her mouth. "I do too," she said, and beamed up at Jesse. He kissed her tenderly. After all, it was a wedding.

Later still, they shared their thoughts and whispers with Michael and Alison. As Michael started to understand, he said, "You two do too?"

Putting the cherry on top of the silliness, Jesse replied, "Wasn't he a character in the Star Wars saga?"

The four, these best of friends, hugged and kissed, made congratulations and plans to get together. They beamed with joy and happiness. Alison placed her hand on Beverly's abdomen as their eyes locked. It felt like a spiritual blessing.

August 23, 2025

Greg was certain their luck had run out. He and Jennifer were accosted by a warlord's gang in Central Alabama after a week of uneventful walking. Along the way they had met some good people and experienced their generosity. On day three they spent an entire day in the Bankhead National Forrest, mostly lounging on outcroppings by a waterfall. They read aloud the poetry of Leonard Cohen to each other. *Tell me again when the rest of the culture has passed through the eye of the camp.*

That night they were enthralled by the dark sky experience of no light pollution. The clear sky shown with the Milky Way and, if magnified, amazing clusters of distant galaxies. Lying on the cool late summer grass of an open field, they had unzipped and spread wide their sleeping bag. All Greg could see was the spiritual wonder of it all, and he could see Jennifer.

They rolled onto their sides, facing each other. Their arms pulled each other close as they lay pelvis to pelvis, mouth to mouth. They stayed that way, melting into each other. Greg rolled slowly on top and Jennifer welcomed him by arching up to meet him. They took off their clothes and relished the cool August breeze. They kissed again and sank to the sleeping bag quilt. Hours passed there, under the stars.

Days of walking brought them to Centreville, Alabama. They had breakfast and headed south through the Cahaba River National Wildlife Refuge. It was there that they were surrounded by gang members.

Six men on motorcycles surrounded Greg and Jennifer on the otherwise empty road. Gasoline was rare and expensive, so this was no chance

229

encounter. Another eight men appeared from a pine thicket to join the others. They threatened Greg with death and Jennifer with gang rape if they couldn't come up with ransom demands in gold bullion.

Jennifer scoffed at the demands. "Just kill us now," she told the men. "We have nothing, and nobody we know has anything. Do you think we would be *here* if we had gold?"

They were taken to headquarters at an abandoned archeology site. The main feature was a kiln from the Brierfield Iron Works. It served as a gathering place for tribal activities. The discussion took a hopeful turn when some members expressed a desire to lighten up. Things were beginning to get better and they were tiring of constant violence and mayhem. The gang of outlaws were not hardened to the circumstances in which they now found themselves. They like everyone else were just trying to survive in a world turned on its head. After deliberations gelled around issues of guilt and innocence, the group voted to let them go on their way, but not before they tried to convince them to stay.

The times they were a changin'... for the better. Morality was revealing itself more often. It was a palpable trend, no longer surprising. Greg and Jennifer were released rather than being conscripted. Jennifer's native kindness and warmth won the day, but it didn't hurt that Jennifer had celebrity status as a former tennis pro.

September 1, 2025

Beverly awoke rested after a good night's sleep. She dined over a cool glass of water. Jesse was out. Her legs were moist. Her water had "broke".

She experienced her first contraction about an hour previously, in her sleep. She had gone back to sleep, twice, then a third contraction got her up and started on her way. She would bicycle to Dr. Wilson's, but first she would hydrate and change clothes.

Beverly was washing her hair in the sink when Jesse came in. She ran to him and held him tight. He hugged her and asked, "What's up, *wet head*?"

"Water broke, early contractions. Labor has started."

"When do you want to go to Mike's?"

"When the contractions get harder and more regular, about 5 minutes apart. This is my first rodeo, Cowboy, and we could be here all night."

Around 3 o'clock in the afternoon, they gathered their things and loaded them and Beverly into a pedi-cab, left from the old times. Jesse pedaled gently around holes in the pavement and the rocks in the road and felt like he was providing a smooth ride. They were nearly there.

This news traveled faster than a pedi-cab, and Dr. Wilson was on his porch waiting for them. He and Jesse helped Beverly transfer from the pedi-cab to a wheelchair. The ride was smooth as silk as they wheeled her to the ultrasound now delivery room. Beverly stood and pivoted to sit on the table then stretched out comfortably on her back. The cushions were fantastic. Beverly noticed they were waterproof.

Michael raised the steel table to a good height for him to help deliver the baby. Jesse stood in the corner, staying out of the way but keeping his gaze on Beverly. He thought *she's doing okay.*

Michael was all business. "How often are the contractions?" "When did your water break?"

"Have you had any unusual pain or bleeding?" Beverly felt better when all the questions were done and were reassuring. Her initial exam also revealed no problems.

"Did you bring a mix tape?" asked Michael.

"A *what*?" asked Beverly.

"A music tape, or rather a thumb drive with music on it. Would you like me to put some music on? Or would you prefer it quiet?"

"I think no music for now. Thanks, Michael."

Michael opened a paper-wrapped obstetrics bundle with sterile gowns and drapes, instruments. He proceeded to scrub and gown, then draped Beverly with leggings and a large sheet, more for sterility than for modesty. He then set up his sterile worktable. *Now we wait.*

Jesse had been out "to get some air". When he stepped back in, Beverly said, "I'm at eight and a half centimeters. That means I can start pushing soon."

Jesse smiled back at her. Their eyes locked and lingered. Then came another contraction.

Beverly reached 10 cm. dilation and had been pushing with her contractions for a while when

Michael said, "Jesse, you want to deliver your daughter?"

There was a pause. Jesse said, "Tell me what to do."

Michael turned to Beverly. "Is that okay with you?"

"Yes," she said. "Oh, yes. Let's do this."

Michael dumped the contents of another obstetrics package on the sterile table and changed into sterile gloves. He gowned Michael and showed him basic sterility technique.

"Beverly, it's time. We talked about delivery positions, remember? Do you want to be on your side, your back, or what?"

"Back is fine. I'm doing okay."

"I'm going to set up some stirrups, but I don't think we'll need them."

The conversation was interrupted by a round of pushing with another contraction. Beverly would never admit it but she was getting tired.

"Jesse, come on in here." Michael helped him position himself in front of the birth canal and placed his hands how they would need to be. "She's crowning. Look, you can see her scalp. She has dark hair."

"Don't let the head pop. Control the head, Jesse. That's it. Hold it in gently to slow it down so she doesn't tear." Michael's instructions were clear to Jesse, but Michael's hands gently over Jesse's were ever more guiding and reassuring.

He did control the head and she didn't tear. The baby was strong with a clear lusty cry. After Jesse clamped and cut the umbilical cord, Michael took the baby straight to the breast, skin to skin, releasing maternal hormones that would help the uterus clamp down and stop the bleeding. Jesse stayed with Beverly while Michael delivered the placenta. No episiotomy and no tears.

Michael looked up at the couple. "We're done here." They were so very much in love he hated to interrupt. "What is her name?"

Beverly responded, "*Aurora.*"

"The Roman goddess of sunrise whose tears turned into the morning dew," Michael roared his approval. "What a marvelous name. Great joy, you two. Let's get you to a room, Beverly."

Jesse, Beverly, and baby Aurora spent the night in a downstairs bedroom at the Wilson's. The next morning, Alison made pancakes while Michael

236

grilled sausage. They took turns gazing at Aurora – this miracle of life.

Michael took Jesse aside; he had something he wanted to say to him alone. "Jesse, I've been at this a long time. I've seen about all there is to see in the field of medicine and in the situations people find themselves in, and I have some words of wisdom for you."

"Let's hear it, o wise one," Jesse said.

"When a man is born, he spends his life trying to impress women. You do your best to make your mother proud, to live up to certain standards. You come close, but there are areas where you maybe could have done better. Then comes courtship and marriage, and again you come close, but you maybe could do better. But then you have a daughter, and here is a woman for whom you can never fall short. In her eyes you can do no wrong; you will always be loved completely."

"Thanks, Mike. I'll keep that in mind. Love you, man." Jesse hurried back to be with Beverly and Aurora.

"Love you, too, my brother."

September 19, 2025

Jeffrey made a call on a woman, Lila Turner, on the northwest Sanibel coast near the old Captiva Bridge before it had been destroyed by Captiva natives seeking further isolation. He had not been to the Mad Hatter since he destroyed his reputation, by spilling his MOAS, his Mother of All Secrets, his role as arms dealer in the Somalian genocide. Lila lived near the Mat Hatter, now closed and shuttered.

Lila thought she glimpsed a stalker the previous night. After interviewing her, he decided that she saw too much, including his truck that she did not yet know was Jeffrey's other vehicle, decided that she was too great a risk, and killed her

238

with an obvious pleasure in the act. He had bound her, played with her, assaulted her, then killed her in the method of the serial killer. It is not clear at times whether Jeffrey knew he was both killer and sheriff – denial, multiple personality disorder, or psychosis are each a possibility. He would return to open the investigation into her death soon enough, assuming someone found her and reported the murder.

He made note to expand his territory to include Captiva. They were probably feeling pretty smug about having blown up the bridge and now not being a scene of serial killings like Sanibel was going though. Jeffrey would fix that.

.   .   .   .   .

The rumor spread on Sanibel that on their return voyage, Jesse and Beverly were boarded by pirates who stole the gold. The pirates suspected the shipment because they were clued in by contacts on Cayman who would get a cut of the loot. They were released by the pirates when Jesse plead their case saying that if they let them go, they would simply head back to Cayman for another load of gold. The pirates would get another chance to catch and board them.

Perhaps no one truly believed the rumor, but no one knew for sure either. It spoke to Jesse's nearly folk lore status on the island. It was clear that he brought them together, that he took a beating for them, and he and Beverly risked everything to bail them out with gold.

Jesse led with strength of personality and determination. When people weighed the decision to stay or leave, Jesse was a factor in deciding to stay.

The murders were a factor in deciding to leave. Still some made the choice to stay. Some left. And some arrived to take their place. Things were tough all over.

Lila Turner was well known and loved. The brutality of her death was sickening to all the islanders. Her age (she was in her fifties) was older than previous victims and the northern tip of Sanibel was distant from a scatterplot of the other crime locations. She fell outside the profile patterns for the other victims.

Jennifer and Greg had settled on Cape San Blas and had taken up residence in the abandoned state park at its tip. They were accepted by the locals because they had a plausible story, were healthy enough to work hard, and could contribute to the settlement's success. The group leader in welcoming them seemed to express doubts that they could adhere to the prevalent group-think. He planned to keep an eye on them.

Jennifer opened hearts and minds by immediately getting to work cleaning the tennis courts and offering free lessons to the area's children. Grateful mothers brought her bread and

241

fresh gulf fish in exchange for the lessons. Greg took on chores as a very capable handy man. They camped behind the dunes, with tarps stretched between the pines. It was a good period of time for them, but they still thought of Sanibel, and wondered.

One very rainy day, they huddled beneath the tarps but still managed to get soaked. "This is not our ultimate destination," said Greg. "I agree," said Jennifer as she snuggled closer to her man.

. . . . .

On Sanibel, Jeffrey Rogers made a show of investigating the murders. He re-interviewed neighbors of victims. He patrolled visibly at dusk when people were out and could be re-assured by his presence. He conferred frequently with Dr. Wilson and Jesse and reported to the council. He kept Russell busy investigating tips and clues to nowhere. He smiled inwardly with self-satisfaction at his cleverness. Tonight, he would kill again. It was time to express the urge.

Book Three

244

September 28, 2025

With reliable electric power and a constant water supply, things began looking up on Sanibel. The crops that survived the hurricane – potatoes, tomatoes, corn, and other vegetables – were starting to come in with some abundance. Chicken and especially fish were adequate, but not abundant.

Jesse and Beverly were cocooning with newborn Aurora. They were rarely seen out. Friends brought groceries. Alison brought cookies for them, and a package of new cloth diapers for little Aurora.

"We will set up a meal train so you won't need to cook for a few days," said Alison. "And Mike and I will bring in dinner soon, too."

.　　.　　.　　.　　.

Greg and Jennifer took jobs on a fishing boat from Cape San Blas. Greg cut bait and threw out the lines and nets. Jennifer was the cook and cleaner for the crew. Some days the catch was too small to meet the high price of gasoline. The crew got I.O.U.s but no other pay other than a fish for dinner. The dense populations of fish near the shore were gone. There was simply not enough oxygen in the water and the effect on fish near the shore was disorientation and death.

Further out, healthy fish could be found, but the cost in time and fuel was prohibitive. The multi-generation family fishing business was failing. Art, don't call him Arthur, and his brother Bart, don't call him Bartholomew, were all ears when Greg told them about the fishing off Sanibel. Greg even offered to show them some good spots in the gulf waters off Sanibel.

246

The next day they caught a grouper. One of the great fish in the Gulf of Mexico. The crew was elated. Spirits ran high. That night at the Captain's table, the wine was choice, and Jennifer's fare included fresh grouper, a generous portion that didn't go into the freezer. Greg was at the Captain's table. The captain wanted to know more. An empty chair was set at the table, presumably for the chef.

Jennifer presented a *Stracciatella*, a spinach egg-drop soup. She ladled out the dish into china bowls. The men were in awe.

"This looks amazing," said Greg.

"Amen to that," added Captain Art.

The Johnson brothers, Art and Bart, were easy to tell apart, despite their close ages. Bart was the one with his left ear missing. "Shark got it," Art told Greg a few days ago.

"Shall I dish a third bowl or wait?" asked Jennifer.

Art said, "Let's wait a few minutes to see if my reclusive brother Bart will join us. I suspect not, but he's known for surprises too; so, maybe. If he does then we'll need another setting."

"I'll have my soup in the kitchen and join you when the grouper's ready, then, if that works," said Jennifer. "Come to the kitchen if Bart gets here, and I'll get him a bowl of soup. And there's plenty if anyone wants seconds."

"Yes, please," the men said in unison.

Jennifer returned with a server's tray held over her head with her right hand and controlling the door with her left hand – a remarkable feat on a rolling ship. She swung the tray to an empty table. She served the soups to the men and to herself as she sat to join them.

"The sauce is reduced about as far as it needs to be," she said.

They ate in a comfortable quiet.

Jennifer retrieved her tray and went back into the galley. Three plates were laid out with crumbled bacon on a bed of sautéed spinach. She got a fresh plate and took a fourth of the spinach bed from each of the three other plates. She plated a generous piece of baked grouper on the spinach bed, ladled on the citrus-chardonnay-cream sauce with crab meat and saffron, and topped it all off with halved grapes.

She was exiting the galley as Bart entered the dining area from the other door. She presented the fish to Art, then Greg. They seemed stunned by beauty of the presentation.

Jennifer looked up at Bart. "Hope you like fish," she teased the man who ate little else. "Where are you sitting?"

Bart took the spot next to his brother and gratefully received the grouper. Jennifer retreated to the galley and returned with Bart's soup, *her* fish dish, and a fresh bottle of their best wine.

They ate in quiet, savoring the flavors, engaging in chit-chat. After dinner they went on deck, unfolded some deck chairs, and broke out the Cubans. Jennifer declined a cigar. The night air was clean and cool, with a breeze. They were ready to talk about Sanibel.

"Tell us about Sanibel," said Art.

"What do you already know?" asked Greg.

"Same as most people, I guess." Art paused. "Sanibel was a haven for billionaires. They had a mercenary group and political clout. They hit the mainland disproportionately, you know, militarily, and a massacre got a lot of attention. The boys from Atlanta came down and wiped out their 'Island

Security'. Those left are trying to make it with farming and fishing. Did I miss much?"

"No," said Greg. "That sums up the recent history. Now let's talk about the future. I can introduce you to Barefoot Chuck. Chuck will direct you to the best areas to fish based on satellite data. He is also protecting other areas, such as hatcheries. There is an intentional community and a strong barter economy. They turned their golf courses into community gardens and corn fields."

No one spoke for minutes. The wine and cigar buzz were having a mellowing effect. Bart spoke first. "We'll head south in the morning." The others nodded their approval.

The meeting was over but still the four lingered in their deck chairs, the men with Cuban cigars. Greg had a cognac; the brothers sipped the wine. The tennis pro did not drink. Jennifer sipped an herbal tea.

It had been quiet for at least ten minutes when Jennifer asked, to no one in particular. "What makes you happy?"

Greg answered, "You do."

"Yes, but what other things. Like for me, it's freedom, staying in the moment, enjoying nature and music, things like that."

"...Joy," said Greg, and he found others, "laughter... contentment... peace." The associations were coming faster now. "caring.. relationships.. love.. acceptance.. rest.. service to others.. thoughts.. gratitude.. living in the moment.. appreciating life and beauty."

"Wow. Okay."

Art spoke next. "I think what you do with yourself matters. I think happiness comes from finding a life that is *meaningful,* maybe in service to others, but still an expression of your gifts."

Not to be outdone, Bart chimed in, "For me deep happiness is keeping balanced and finding what resonates. You have to balance relationships, work, nature, walking and other mind-body-spirit aspects of your life. You have to find what resonates, with positive energy and goodwill."

"To positive energy and goodwill," Greg toasted with his cognac.

Jennifer lifted her cup of tea. The brothers smiled. Everyone got quiet again.

251

After another conversational lull, Greg asked Art and Bart why they decided to go to Sanibel.

Bart answered, "I do most of the bookkeeping for the fishing business. Fishing was a solid revenue stream for most of our lives, and we've done well. Lately we just cannot move product for the prices fish used to fetch, which is good in a way because of how far you must go now to find fish. Bottom line is, we are bankrupt and in debt to a Port St. Joe lender. We best not go back. He could take our boat."

October 2, 2025

The fishing continued to improve the further south they went on the *S. S. Minnow*. (The Johnson brothers had a sense of humor.) Another day of good catches and the freezer would be full. They headed for Sanibel; it was time for Art and Bart to meet Barefoot Chuck.

After a few days at sea, the *Minnow* docked at the Port of Sanibel where the causeway had once united the island with the mainland. They were disappointed to not see Chuck among those on the pier. When they told the man who came to help them dock about their hold full of fish, they were told that they might want to take the catch on over to the ice plant. "Punta Gorda Fish and Ice over on Pine Island will give you a good price."

Art thanked the man and the crew shoved off for the quick trip west across Pine Island Sound. When they returned they all had gold from the sale of the fish. For Jennifer and Greg it was more than fair wages. For Art and Bart it was a fresh start. This time when the *Minnow* docked, Barefoot Chuck was there to meet them. Art and Bart were disappointed to see that Chuck actually did wear shoes like anybody else. The name came from a story for another time.

Chuck set the brothers to go out in two or three days to test the waters. Meanwhile they would look for housing near the boat yard. Greg and Jennifer needed a place to stay as well, so they all headed down the road to the Visitor Center building. There they were processed, and added to the census, still a work in progress. They were told to look around for a place and if they found something, make sure it was structurally safe, then come back to the "Visitor Center" and claim it for the records. They were told to check at the library for ways to contribute.

"Other than that, just don't kill anyone," said the perky twenty-something lady at the desk. She had meant it as a way of saying 'that's how easy it

254

is', or just 'be good', but she could see from the shocked expressions on the people around the room, that her remark had crossed a line.

Greg and Jennifer sensed the silent, tense scene and asked what's going on.

"I am sorry for my choice of words," said the woman. "There is no newspaper, so I guess I better tell you. There has been a series of murders on Sanibel, some joggers, all women. Several people are helping the Sheriff but so far, not much. Just be alert out there. Okay? You fit the profile, Jennifer."

Jennifer nodded, "Thanks for the heads up."

.   .   .   .   .

Alison knocked and Beverly opened the door to let her and Michael into the house. They had brought dinner, half prepared, to finish in Beverly and Jesse's kitchen.

The first thing they did was to peek in on one-month-old baby Aurora, sleeping in her crib. Then they settled in for the evening visit. Dinner flowed from light prep, to oven time, choice of wine to pair, setting the table, eating something delicious,

255

and clean-up. By the time they settled in the living room, they were ready to settle somewhere, anywhere.

The long-time friends fell into a comfortable silence. Jesse was seeing to the wine refills. Beverly was taking advantage of no longer being pregnant, and indulging with the others for a change.

"What's it like for you, being new parents and all?" asked Alison. "I know you are thrilled; you both just glow."

"It's indescribable," said Beverly.

"It's life changing," added Jesse. "Life affirming, too."

A whimpering cry came from Aurora's room and Beverly left to breast feed her daughter.

"Life affirming," Michael mused. "Often, people find children to be a reason to affirm that life is worth living."

"Do you wonder sometimes?"

"Yes. I think we all do. But it helps beyond measure to find someone with whom you can share your concepts of life and talk freely, be authentic. Live your life with integrity and stay true to whatever world view you can come up with. You know?" Michael look over at Alison and mouthed, "Love you."

"This whole 'bringing life into the world thing' is unsettling," said Jesse. "What if that was the wrong thing to do? The problems are real. Was this the *wise* thing to do?"

Michael saw an opportunity to quote Confucius. Raising a finger in the air, he waxed professorial: "By three methods we may learn wisdom: First, by reflection, which is noblest; second, by imitation, which is easiest; and third by experience, which is the bitterest."

"Your values are good;" Michael continued. "Aurora's will be too. She will grow to find the beauty in nature and in relationship with others. You did right to bring this child into the world."

"Thanks for that. All I know is I love her and will do anything to protect her."

October 28, 2025

Three weeks later, at Michael and Alison's house, they were at it again. Talking about anything and everything; sated from grilled vegetables and redfish.

"I was born into money, thus I had the luxury of being able to major in philosophy, but also I had a cyber security start-up, right place right time, and then I negotiated the collapse. So, yeah, now I'm in a position where I can help Sanibel, whatever remains of her."

Beverly had finally gotten around to asking Jesse more about the origins of his riches, and it so happened to be when they were visiting Michael and Alison. She asked, "What do you mean 'luxury'?"

"Well a Ph.D. in philosophy doesn't lead to a lucrative path," replied Jesse. "There's a job prospects joke that ends with 'Would you like fries with that?'"

"Changing the subject," Michael chimed in, "where are we on this 'helping Sanibel' thing?"

"Okay, well we're funded for now, but we need to expand income streams to be self-sustaining. I think the place is coming together. The hurricane set us back, but some crops came through. We lost structures but not communities. Friendships have strengthened and people are pulling together."

"I can vouch for what Michael is saying," said Alison. "A community feast of Friendsgiving is about to take place. This one is for real gratitude. We will have the traditional socializing the fourth Thursday of November, but this one's for real, driven by love and respect for each other, not by the calendar."

"There's more to restoring Sanibel to wholeness," said Michael. "We have a killer on the loose. I am tired of doing autopsies on young women."

"We *have* a pattern," said Jesse flatly.

"Indeed we do," agreed Michael.

259

"What else do we know, besides the victims are all young adult women?" asked Beverly. Jesse still did not know about the attack on her, and her out-running the attacker.

"Two were joggers," Jesse replied first. "Three were home invasions, and two more were staged to look like home invasions. There were no clues at the crimes, any of them, that gave us anything new, nothing to follow up on anyway. Jogging attacks were away from structures, but around trees, so that makes me think he stalks with a deer hunter's tree stand. The one outlier is Lila Turner. She was older, and like Marti, it was staged to look like a home invasion. Actually, both Lila and Marti could have let the killer in, as if he were someone trusted. And then there is the kill technique. It looks professional to me. What do you make of it, Michael?"

"The necks were broken cleanly, but that was a post-mortem signature. "The fatal blow in each case was a six-inch serrated blade to the heart, followed by 2 or 3 gratuitous stab wounds to the chest and liver. We had already deduced that the killer was male, now we can recognize a military technique, Special Forces maybe"

260

"And don't forget crazy," added Beverly.

"Yes," continued Michael. "He is likely psychopathic – a malignant narcissist who feels rejected, by lovers, women he cannot have, by friends he can no longer confide in. He is a man who feels betrayed, and he wants his vengeance."

Jesse spoke, "Give it some time. He will make a mistake and we will get him."

"Do we have any suspects?" asked Alison. "Any at all?"

"None officially," answered Michael.

"Yes, well I can add to the profile," Beverly confessed. "He can run nearly as fast as I can." Beverly and the Wilsons told Jesse the story of her escape from an attempted attack by our killer. Jesse was upset that they had not told him right away, but also relieved that Beverly and the baby had not been hurt.

"I know you didn't see his face, but whose face do you see when you relive this in your dreams?" asked Michael.

"Who do you all see?" Beverly asked, looking at each. "Who do you know on this island who has the skill set, the temperament, the weird crazy streak? Who do you see?"

261

They looked at each other as if they were figuring things out *en masse.*

Jeffrey! They each thought.

"Jeffrey," said Beverly out loud. "I see Jeffery in my nightmares."

"We have no proof," cautioned Alison.

"None yet," agreed Jesse. "Like I said, he will make a mistake. Maybe now we know where to look. Maybe Russell could tail him on his night patrol."

"And be careful."

November 11, 2027

Everyone seemed jubilant; happy to be with neighbors for Sanibel's first Friendsgiving celebration, two weeks before Thanksgiving. This feast was for gratitude, for life and friendship, "driven by love and respect for each other, not by the calendar," as Alison had said.

Jennifer and Greg showed up at the dinner, recently having arrived from Cape San Blas by boat, and eager to hook up with old friends. Jesse and Beverly brought a ham from their freezer. Alison and Michael were playing hostess and host in the spacious downstairs of the library. Liz Forbes arrived with Lucy Cochran and Mercedes Phillips; now the party would get going.

Barefoot Chuck said he counted 134 people at the potluck gathering. There was music. Amateurs no more. Many local people had hidden talents and instruments of every stripe. The poetess with a jazz saxophone backup band was the crowd favorite. High energy rock rated highly, too.

The crowd spilled out onto the courtyard and toward the marina from there. Jeffrey kept an eye on the party from the periphery. He didn't think he would be missed.

Jesse took advantage of the assembled crowd to organize a militia for the purpose of finding the killer. The liberal-minded of the community were losing the debate about vigilante-justice.

Jennifer, Beverly, Alison, Lucy, Mercedes, and Liz were dancing mercilessly, moving hard core to the rock and ska, swaying seductively to the bluesy jazz.

Michael and Greg were catching each other up on the news of the year. Adventures in Tennessee, Alabama, and Florida yielded to murders and mainland intrigue in Sanibel.

"Jesse really did all that?" Greg asked when Michael fished telling his tale.

"It's somethin', isn't it?"

"Truly it is." And they were silent for a while before they drifted to the music and dancing.

November 17, 2025

Monday meetings were getting more routine, but nothing was easy. The mainland council requested Jesse to meet with them about new trade agreements. It appeared to be positive, and they guaranteed his safety and protection. He would leave in the morning.

That evening Jesse packed some papers. Beverly asked him if he would take a lunch, and they agreed it would be a good idea. Jesse said he wanted to post Deputy McGee outside her door.

"Russell is a big man with a good heart. I would feel better with someone keeping an eye on you while I'm in Fort Myers."

"No argument here," said the new mother.

.　　.　　.　　.　　.

The next morning Beverly packed a lunch for Jesse while he met outside with Russell McGee. Russell found a shady spot under a banyan tree and set up his folding chair.

Jesse and Beverly said their 'good-byes' in the bedroom. Baby Aurora was sleeping soundly as Jesse watched lovingly. After a while, he said, "Time to go."

Jesse pedaled his Litespeed to the pier where Chuck was waiting. Chuck took Jesse to Fort Myers on his fishing boat with a crew of five. He waited as Jesse negotiated trade terms. During Jesse's diplomatic mission in Fort Myers, Chuck met with the fish mongers and built some new business relationships. They left earlier than either thought they would. Things just went smoothly.

When they were docking at the pier, Jesse bolted as soon as the ship was close enough to the landing. He had told Chuck that it was just a bad feeling, but that was all Jesse needed.

. . . . .

Jesse leapt on his bicycle and sped toward home. Moments earlier, Jeffrey had walked up to Russell, in the shade, under the banyan tree.

"Let me spell you for a few hours," Jeffrey offered.

"Can't," replied Russell. "Gave my word."

"You could use a power nap," said Jeffrey. "You look tired."

"I'm alright, Jeffrey," said the deputy. "I can stay up for days on end."

Jeffrey stepped forward and made a show of putting his left hand on Russell's shoulder. "Good job," he said. He squeezed the shoulder.

Russell winced from the shoulder squeeze. *It was deliberately too hard; painful. Distracting. Meant to be distracting.*

As Jeffrey pulled Russell toward him, he thrust his military knife through Russell's epigastrium and into his left cardiac ventricle. He was dead instantly, so the neck fracture was just an exercise, an old habit. Jeffrey turned his attention to the house. *Any more guards?*

When Jeffrey appeared at Beverly and Jesse's front door, he rang the video doorbell. Beverly answered and indicated the house would stay locked until Jesse got back from his trade mission. Jeffrey's demeanor quickly became threatening and with Aurora in the house, Beverly felt particularly vulnerable. *Where is Russell? I want Jesse!*

Jeffrey was shouting and rambling on about *traitors and turncoats*, and the Mad Hatter, ranting and pounding on the other side of the sturdy steel door, leading Beverly to understand that they were right that night. "NSA Agent" Jeffrey Rogers was a professional killer in a previous life, and that he was behind the Sanibel murders. Jeffrey's agitated ramblings made it clear that he blamed Jesse for Sanibel's and his (Jeffrey's) downfall through some irrational logic stream that began the night of the Mad Hatter dinner and the battle of Sanibel, that he resented Jesse for escaping the carnage, and that the

269

best way to extract revenge would be to kill the woman Jesse loves and his newborn child.

Jeffrey was desperate to find a way into the house – steel doors and hurricane shutters, the stucco might as well have been concrete. He went to the garage peered through the garage door windows. *There!* He saw the chink in the armor.

Jeffrey broke out a garage door window easily. The opening in the steel door was too small for a person to crawl through, but Jeffrey could insert his right arm to the shoulder. And with that reach, he could just touch the release handle for the garage door. He tapped it repeatedly to set it to swinging, and at the end of its arc, Jeffrey grabbed the handle. With an easy steady pull, he felt the 'pop' of the door releasing from the mechanism that mechanically raises the door and locks the garage when it's closed. *Released.* Jeffrey quietly raised the door, stepped in and closed the garage door behind him. He reattached the garage door to the door opener and cut the release cord. *Now everybody is locked out.*

Jesse cycled into the neighborhood in time to glimpse a shadowy form near the garage. He rode up the driveway and came to a stop at the garage door. He found Russell's body near the banyan tree; killed with Jeffrey's signature cardiac wound. Peering through the garage window, he could see the cut release cord and could surmise the rest. Jesse began to panic.

Beverly and the baby are in there. Jeffrey is in there with them. Jesse ran to the front door, tested it. *Locked.* Jesse hadn't needed keys before. *There was a hiding place for a spare key. But where? Beverly changes it. Where was the last place? Around back in the garden. Beverly! This is time I don't have!*

One interior door was locked between Jeffrey and his targets: Beverly and Aurora. Jeffrey looked at the door that separated the home addition from the main house. It was locked with a classic hardware key-set. Jeffrey put a military boot heel through the key-set, splintering the door frame. He entered the kitchen from the den. *Now, where would I hide myself and a baby? Upstairs bathroom? One more lock.*

Jeffrey climbed the stairs and stood outside the bathroom door. "Beverly, if I can kick open the door downstairs, I can easily kick this one open, and it will wake the baby."

271

Beverly was helpless with Aurora in her arms. Jeffrey had led them out of the bathroom into the bedroom, where he let her sit on the bed holding her baby. As he threatened Beverly with a knife, brandishing it theatrically, Jeffrey revealed that he recently dispatched Beverly's friend Marti the same way. *She was worthless and no fun since the Mad Hatter dinner anyway.*

Jesse found the rock with the hidden key. He ran to the front door and left it open to attract help. He grabbed a knife from the kitchen and moved stealthily 2 steps at a time up to the bedroom. He heard a man's voice.

Beverly listened quietly. Jeffrey seemed to be off in his own little world. Ranting would ordinarily be something to avoid, but now Beverly made herself look attentive – a rapt student. Jesse kept talking. Beverly was pulling a reverse Scheherazade.

Jesse crashed into the room wielding a substantial butcher knife. He knocked Jeffrey off-balance, and had the element of surprise, but the fight was unbalanced. Jeffrey was a trained killer and a psychopath; Jesse was a Doctor of Philosophy trained in of all the worthless (at the moment) fields,

272

philosophy. The fight was not going well. They each had knives, and each got in some cuts, some deeper than others. If Jesse were not fighting for Beverly and the child, he could not have kept up the effort given the repeated wounds Jeffrey inflicted.

The struggle continued with Beverly trying to help, but Jeffrey knocked her down, stunned momentarily. He seemed to be growing in confidence that he could take them both. *I might enjoy toying with them first,* Jeffrey thought smugly. *Let them cringe while I toy with that baby,*

He's distracted, Jesse thought. *He has made a mistake.* As Jeffrey continued in his daydream, Beverly quietly stood up behind the bed on which Aurora was still sleeping, opposite where Jesse and Jeffrey struggled on the floor. She unplugged a large Himalayan salt lamp that was on the dresser and swung it with fury onto Jeffrey's skull, stunning *him.* Jeffrey's grip on Jesse's wrist relaxed.

Jesse killed him with the killer's own signature move: a stab wound through the upper stomach, a pivot toward the neck, and a thrust into the heart ventricle. Jesse had learned it well from all those months of investigation. Distracted by a reverie of cruelty, no more fitting or ironic end could have come to the bastard.

Jesse crawled to Beverly and she cleansed his wounds, and Aurora slept. Beverly and Jesse fell together exhausted until Beverly asked, "Is it over."

"It's over," Jesse reassured her. "*Finito.*"

.   .   .   .   .

After a half-hour of lying exhausted on the floor, not far enough from the exsanguinated Jeffrey, Jesse was the first to stir. He had done an inventory of his wounds and the cumulative damage was worse than the sum of its parts. He took Beverly's shoulder and her eyes opened, looking into his for answers.

"We need to get some rest. Let's go to the guest bedroom," he suggested.

"No arguments there, Cowboy."

They somehow made their way to the clean bed, leaning on Aurora's crib as they rolled it the short distance down the hall.

The guest bedroom was well-appointed, spacious, and comfortable – long ago updated from

Brady Chapman's taste. The O'Connell family had no difficulty settling in and falling asleep.

November 19, 2025

Jesse woke often during the night. The pain was bearable only because they had prevailed – prevailed against all odds. Prevailed against all reason. They should all be dead now. Instead, they were survivors.

Not just Jesse, Beverly, and Aurora, but all of Sanibel. The people and the island herself were survivors. They had survived artillery shelling. They had survived starvation level hunger. They had survived loneliness and loss. They had rebuilt only to see it swept away by Hurricane Denise. They rebuilt again. They had survived a serial killer. They pulled together and they had *survived*.

Michael was awakened by his satellite phone. Few people could have made that call.

"Michael, it's Beverly. Oh, Mike, it's a bloody mess here. Jesse's cut up pretty bad. But, Mike! Jeffrey's dead! He attacked us. Jesse's hurt pretty bad. He's in and out."

"On my way!"

.　　.　　.　　.　　.

When Michael arrived at the O'Connells, the door was still open from earlier that night. It was not yet dawn. The lights were on upstairs.

Beverly met him in the upstairs hallway. He helped her back to the bedroom. Beverly had tried to bandage Jesse's wounds and did get most of the bleeding stopped, but she herself had been knocked silly and was still struggling with a post-concussive headache.

Michael bent over Jesse who looked back up at him with a crooked smile. He otherwise was not moving. Blood had run from wounds to pool in the center of the bed. Jesse was pale but not ghostly.

Michael pulled the lower eyelids down with a thumb – pale conjunctivae, but he'd seen worse. A pen light revealed equal and reactive pupils. Grip strength was good bilaterally. No obvious brain trauma. Amazingly, all of the cuts were superficial enough to avoid a fatal outcome. A stab to the chest was blocked from penetrating the heart by a rib just left of the sternum. Ordinarily the knife blade would have dealt the rib a glancing blow on its path to the cardiac ventricle. But in this instance, owing to the razor-sharp tip on Jeffrey Roger's attack knife, the blade tip embedded in the bone. *He would have had to tug at it to free it,* Michael muttered to himself.

"Yeah, I remember that," mused Jesse.

"Yeah, you're going to remember that one a good long while." Michael addressed them both. "I don't believe Tarzan here would much enjoy the trip to my office where I could sew him up. I think I can piece him back together here with what's in my bag. I could use your help Beverly. Feel up to it?"

"Feeling strong, Cap'n."

"I noticed your bandaging techniques. You're well trained."

"Thanks."

"Thanks? That's all I get? How about a story?"

Amused and high on morphine, Jesse pleaded, "Yeah, babe. Tell us a story."

After the cleansing, anesthetizing, and suturing had begun, Beverly started her story: "I'm an R.N."

"I knew it!" said Michael.

"Who-eee," said Jesse. It was hard to know how much he would remember of this.

"So what happened?" Michael asked as they got into the routine of cleaning and suturing.

"I was an ICU nurse at the beginning of the pandemic, Mike, in the thick of it. Night and day, day and night, it was horrible, and then, 6 months into it the case load exploded. That was Covid-19 in 2020; then came hemorrhagic Covid-21. The health care system collapsed when the government did. Pollard was impeached and I honestly don't know who is running things in Washington, do you?"

Michael shook his head, but didn't want to interrupt.

"I became just another refuge during the food riots. I found my way to Sanibel before I knew much about the place. I know how to garden, and I made my way after I got here as well."

They continued to clean wounds and suture. After a quiet period Beverly said, "I hear there were a few new Covid-19 cases popping up after Friendsgiving."

"A few people are still not vaccinated. Can you believe it? I started them on one of the newer antiviral meds. I had samples. They'll be fine; they are isolating."

"What about Jeffrey's body. I would like it out of the house."

"Of course. I will take it with me and do an autopsy. I will submit a report to the council when we meet Monday, since there is no sheriff and no deputy."

"I am so glad you are here, Michael."

"Always."

Jesse was sleeping through his repair. He would stay asleep all day and night. Beverly would rouse him every few hours and check his status and vital signs. Everyone was starting to relax.

November 27, 2025

It was Thanksgiving Day and there was plenty to be thankful for. After surviving the knife fight with Jeffrey, Jesse had been in need of repair. He was pleased and surprised Dr. Wilson was really quite skilled at minor surgery. Jesse was healing well, and some stitches would come out in a few days.

Jesse and Beverly (and Aurora) were hosting the doctor and his bride for Thanksgiving dinner. Jennifer and Greg would arrive soon. They were both so grateful to be alive, and to have Aurora safe

281

and sound; and Michael and Alison were a big part of their lives during this period of destruction and survival, death and life.

When Greg and Jennifer did arrive, Jennifer went to the kitchen to finish preparations. It was a modest spread at the dinner table. Redfish was the main course and Jennifer was the acknowledged master chef. The wine was a Duckhorn sauvignon blanc. The conversations overlapped.

"I never would have thought we would have made it this far; not after the hurricane."

"Damn shame about Jeffrey. But what could we have done even if we had known."

"Vegetable crop has done okay, and next year there should be a surplus."

"We will need a surplus. More people will be staying and arriving, now that the murders are no longer a threat."

"How are you two doing, Beverly? Really? That was a horrible ordeal."

"What is this recipe for the redfish, Jennifer? You must give it to me."

"I think you would have to surmise that the veneer of civilization is very thin."

"*Aurora* is such a beautiful name. How did you come up with it?"

"Fishing is definitely better in this part of the Gulf than it is north of here."

"Greg, the town needs a sheriff. Are you tired of fishing yet?"

"We found some Christmas decorations in the town garage, where we maintained the garbage trucks, firetrucks and police cars. We should put up lights around town or something."

.   .   .   .   .

Away from the holiday gathering, blocks away, on the beach, seagulls cried in the distance. Sandpipers gathered in groups of three and took tentative steps. A lone male sandpiper ran past a bit of driftwood in a streak. Head bobbing, legs a blur. Then one joined him, then another and another. In a flash there were twenty sandpipers running pall-mall toward the surf. They paused at the water's edge, beaks plunging into the soft wet sand, searching for morsels of protein. Heads down, tails straight out, they scurried toward, then away from the gentle surf as it crashed and flowed up the sandy slope, then retreated, leaving a sheet of nutrients in its wake. The excited flock cheeped in concert as they flowed back and forth and swarmed side to side, feeding through the inch-deep water.

Small and darting, the sandpipers were generally ignored by the larger seagulls. Their soft cheeps were no match for the seagull's lusty cry. Grey-patterned wings, a grey irridescent head and cowl, and a soft and downy snow-white chest and belly made this beachcomber beautiful.

The previous year the entire Gulf Coast had been impacted by a cataclysmic red tide. These were the survivors. A bloom of algae, that is toxic to sensitive populations of sea life that feed from the ocean bottom, is toxic to sandpipers, too. Miles of dead fish that littered the beaches in 2024 got all the attention because of the bad odor and eye irritation. Manatees, dolphins, and hundreds of sea turtles washed up dead on the shores. It was a smelly mess. But the red tide left its mark on Florida's birds, too. Sandpipers, especially, are more sensitive to the changes in their food supply.

Sandpipers and seagulls alike took to chasing a small crab. The sandpipers lost the competition and searched eagerly for the next bite of food. Every day was Thanksgiving for these creatures.

The skies filled with flutters of white as the girl walked through their midst. Taking flight with the others to escape the feet coming through the flocks, dozens of sandpipers and seagulls scattered, forming a great wave of birds as if the sea were parting for Moses.

December 15, 2027

Lucy Cochran surprised everyone with her announcement that she would challenge Greg for the position of sheriff. Greg said he would rather fish than stand in her way.

Barefoot Chuck looked pleased. He anticipated the return of a sea captain with skills.

Doctor Wilson said that with no new Covid-19 and none, *none!*, of the hemorrhagic Covid-21 at all, he was pleased to declare the quarantine successful, the outbreaks following Friendsgiving and Thanksgiving contained, and the lockdown lifted. Gatherings can occur now, he added, but only outdoors. Limit distances to 8 feet and wear a washable face mask, black and cut to fit. Last, the autopsy on Jeffrey Rogers revealed death due to a stab wound to the heart.

Barefoot Chuck spoke next. "Damn, Doc, that's great news. But this here's the thing: I've never once seen you say so much with so few words. You know what I mean?" he teased. "You usually just drone on and on."

He looks around at the others to say, "You usually can't shut him up!" The other council members laughed, but only because the joke applied to them as well.

"I'll call on the rest of us in a few minutes, but first I wanted to say that this can be the last Monday morning council meeting for the year."

The split screen images were nodding in agreement and approval. The screen image went full on Chuck when he resumed talking.

"So with things smoothing out and Christmas coming, we can finish out the year's business and meet back again in January." Again the members could be seen nodding in agreement.

"I have *Lucy Cochran* in nomination for sheriff. We need a motion to appoint her to the office of sheriff."

"So move," said Jesse.

"Second."

"Discussion?... Seeing none, voice vote?" A chorus of *ayes* sealed the deal.

"Lucy? May I be the first to congratulate you. May I call you *Sheriff Cochran*?"

"Lucy is fine, or sheriff. You know what? I don't really care which," she said with a broad smile.

The other council members contributed with reports and updates. Jesse seemed to follow every presentation and contributed to some. He was glad though, that Barefoot Chuck was handling the agenda so capably. It would make his announcement much easier. Jesse was last to speak.

"Before I take my turn, what happen to that poker cheat, Henry Farber? The former mayor? Has anyone heard anything?"

"I have," offered Lucy Cochran. "I know perhaps more than I should."

"Tell us," they asked. "Where has Henry been?"

"When Alderman invaded Sanibel, it was chaos. Henry ran north on foot, past the bird sanctuary. He wasn't seen or heard from. Hell, we thought a gator got him. Where it turns out he

288

turned up was up north of Bowman's Beach, in the bogs near Silver Key."

"I didn't know anyone was still there. Some abandoned homes in bad shape, maybe," said Chuck.

"Turned out Henry found the only person living out there, Chester Frist – Crazy Chester, they call him. Chester told Henry he didn't need him or want him in the house with him. Henry said he would work, do anything. Henry was still in shock from the bombings and thought all of Sanibel was gone."

"Chester told Henry he could stay and be Chester's man servant, but he had to cook and clean. Chester said Henry could sleep in the bombed out house next door and he would help him put it in the dry, but he couldn't sleep in Chester's condo. No sir!"

"So that is how Henry Farber, the mayor of Sanibel, became Crazy Chester's man servant."

It was Jesse's turn to present to the council. He announced that he would be taking some paternity leave. He would also be healing for a while, but he would return in the Spring.

"You all have been so important to me, so inspirational. Thank you all so very much."

With that the council stood as one and applauded, slowly, respectfully.

Jesse was pleased but embarrassed also. His humility was genuine.

December 25, 2027

It was Christmas Day. Michael awoke to breakfast in bed and gave Alison a tubular wrapped present from behind his bed.

As she neatly unwrapped the gift, her eyes opened wider and she asked, "Where did you find this?"

"I've had it since I was a teen," said Michael. "It was the first play I saw."

In the last two months, Alison had, with help from Lucy Cochran, reinvigorated the Community Theater. She and Lucy had staged *Man of La Mancha*, and Michael had just gifted his wife with an original 1972 movie poster, starring Peter O'Toole and Sophia Loren.

Greg and Jennifer had been up late and slept late. Sanibel was working well for them and they were a welcome addition to the community. Greg Johnston presented Jennifer Marin with a ring and she accepted instantly and emotionally. They would not be going out any time soon.

Jesse and Beverly were completely fulfilled. Aurora would be four months old in a week. Baby Aurora was given the poetic name of the Roman goddess of sunrise whose tears turned into the morning dew, as Michael had informed them on her birth day. Disney's Sleeping Beauty, Aurora, would be sure to make any little girl feel like a princess, but she was no match for the sleeping beauty that was Aurora O'Connell.

The radiant sleeping Aurora is also associated with the term for the Northern Lights; The joy that she had brought to Jesse and Beverly was more vast than the heavens.

Aurora Leigh was the name of an epic poem by Elizabeth Barrett Browning. She wrote this prescient verse in Book 9:

It is the hour for souls;
That bodies, leavened by the will and love,
Be lightened to redemption. The world's

old;

But the old world waits the hour to be renewed:

Toward which, new hearts in individual growth

Must quicken, and increase to multitude

In new dynasties of the race of men,—

Developed   whence,   shall   grow spontaneously

New churches, new economies, new laws

Admitting   freedom,   new   societies

Excluding falsehood. HE shall make all new.

.   .   .   .   .

The baby cooed when Jesse held her and looked into her eyes. He knew that things truly would be better from this time on. Her name, *Aurora Leigh,* symbolized a new beginning.

293

December 30, 2027

Jesse was atop *Serenity*, rocked by the moon and its tide, and by the stars upon which he gazed. Beverly and Aurora were asleep in the cabin below deck. He was at peace. He had a strange thought.

The UFOs! The bright lights and their fast movements, abrupt disappearances, and hoverings – especially the hoverings – that people around the Florida coast see all the time. What if the sightings not of aliens at all, but a distortion in the homogeneity of the balance of energy, matter, dark matter, and dark energy. The cosmic microwave background radiation is dramatically homogenous throughout the universe. In the beginning, after only 10^{-37} seconds, exponential growth smoothed out nearly all irregularities. Small distortions,

294

anisotropies, do exist and could produce curious light displays. Heat does surge... light may spark... gravity can distort; and we see it as a freaky phenomenon over Florida's coastline. With partial information we fill in the rest – UFOs.

He looked up at the Milky Way in a brilliance of stars. He drifted further into a gnostic state, an altered state of consciousness in which the mind is focused on only one point, and all other thoughts are thrust out. *And beyond your core is the South Pole Wall, an outer arm of countless galaxies. And beyond you all is Laniakea, our home supercluster. And beyond that are other superclusters. And beyond the known universe are other universes, flashing into existence with white-hot plasma and fading into oblivion over hundreds of billions of years – not unlike a lightening bug signaling for a mate.* Jesse was merging into the oneness of creation.

As he meditated, he shed his *individual* nature, he cleared his mind, but only after atonement. He recommitted to the forces of life and love. He praised his Maker. He rededicated his energies to fostering sapience

295

among the Sapiens. Jesse did not knowingly do these things, rather they represented deeper forces awake in his being. He was Awake when he entered the Cloud of Unknowing.

It is a burden to be sentient, to be conscious and aware that your particular unit of stardust is aware of the universe, thus the *universe* is aware of itself. Not only is your stardust unit terribly finite regarding lifespan, your species appears hell-bent toward extinction. Not only is your stardust unit aware of its own existence, you are also aware that your existence will cease, just like the universe and everything else. That is a burden worthy of the Serenity Prayer.

A firm splash of wave against the side of the boat brought Jesse back to focus on the things around him. He got up and climbed down the ladder to the cabin. He found Beverly curled around Aurora in the cabin bed. He slipped out of his shirt and shorts and joined them. Snuggling up against Beverly, he regained the arms of Morpheus.

The End